The
Resurrection
Chronicles

Mike MacCarthy

outskirts press

Author's Note:

- Many who have read early versions of *The Resurrection Chronicles* have raised questions about my sources. That's why I've included such a detailed bibliography.

- A note about the "Days" you will find in each new heading and chapter. It requires over half the book to explain all that was taking place on the "First Day," which is the day of the Resurrection of Jesus Christ from His tomb.

- World acclaimed British author and theologian, C. S. Lewis, is reported to have said, "We read to know we're not alone." But then in the movie *Verdict* (1982), a sincere lawyer played by Paul Newman tells his jury, "So much of the time we're just lost. We say, 'Please, God, tell us what is right; tell us what is true'. . . . And we become tired of hearing people lie."

So what are we to think about the written word? Is it largely a pack of lies or is it most often a gift from a heartfelt author who really wants to help us know? I believe that the written word can be a "fervent and frightened prayer" (Newman's words in the *Verdict*) that lifts us out of our loneliness and helps us know.

My hope is that you find *The Resurrection Chronicles* to be such a prayer.

Dedication:

This book and all that has gone into its creation and production is dedicated to the Blessed Virgin Mary, who asks to be thought of as a mother to each of us, and is sometimes referred to as Our Mother of Perpetual Help. And so we pray:

Remember, O most gracious Virgin Mary, that never was it known that anyone who fled to thy protection, implored thy help, or sought thy intercession, was left unaided. Inspired by this confidence, we fly unto thee, O Virgin of Virgins, our Mother. To thee we come, before thee we stand, sinful and sorrowful. O Mother of the Word Incarnate, despise not our petitions, but in thy mercy, hear and answer us. Amen

Table of Contents

Introduction

One cannot truly appreciate the events that took place beginning with the Crucifixion of Jesus and ending with Pentecost, without considering the political conditions and religious and cultural practices of Jewish life under Roman rule at that time. I have included here a brief explanation in hopes of increasing understanding for the reader. The people discussed here are all real.

THE POLITICS OF JERUSALEM AT THE TIME OF JESUS:

When Mary gave birth to Jesus, Augustus Caesar had been in power since 27 BC. His rule fomented fear and paranoia throughout the realm as a means of control—especially in Judea and Jerusalem. For the City of David and its environs, three hubs of power and turmoil translated into a daily reminder for the Jewish people of their complete subjugation: the Herod dynasty, the Roman governor, and the Temple men and the Jewish High Council, known as the Sanhedrin.

KING HEROD ANTIPAS:

Since Jesus and His parents lived in Nazareth, King Herod Antipas had technical legal authority over their lives. The Herodian dynasty began with Herod the Great, who assumed the throne of Judea with Roman support in 37 BC. Herod's kingdom ended in 4 BC, when it became a Tetrarchy and the power was divided among his four sons. Herod Antipas was awarded power over Galilee and

Perea (aka Peraea, see diagram below) which played a significant role in the trial of Jesus.

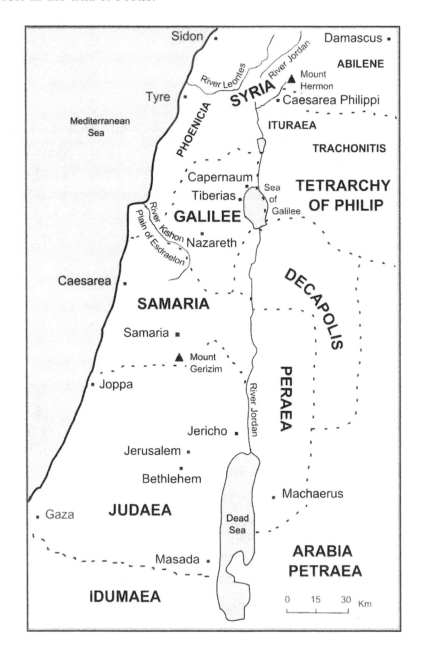

Roman Governor

In 26 A.D. the Roman Emperor Tiberius appointed Pontius Pilate governor of the Roman province of Judaea, which included Jerusalem. As a governor, Pontius Pilate had the power of a supreme judge, which meant that only he had the authority to order a criminal execution. His duties also included other routine tasks such as overseeing tax collection and managing construction projects. But his most crucial responsibility was that of maintaining law and order.

The Temple Men

At the time Jesus lived, there were four major sects of Judaism: Pharisees, Essenes, Zealots, and Sadducees. The Pharisees in New Testament times were deeply committed to moral behavior and a scholarly approach to Scripture. Their stance on morality included a rigid adherence to behavioral aspects of Mosaic Law. However, since some of those laws were vague, the Pharisees developed an "Oral Torah"—a set of traditions that created a buffer zone around the Law of Moses that ensured piety. The Pharisees also believed in a literal afterlife and the bodily resurrection of the dead.

The Essenes were a monastic group. Unlike the other sects, these Jews felt called to separate from Jewish society in preparation for the end of the world. In broad strokes, the Essenes could be considered a doomsday sect. They felt the end times were imminent, and it was their duty to patiently and passively await the apocalypse.

On the other side of the apocalyptic coin were the Zealots, by far the smallest of the four groups. Like the Essenes, the Zealots were something of a doomsday sect of Judaism. However, the Zealots believed their actions would directly influence when and how this apocalypse occurred. Specifically, they believed they were called to commit acts of violence against the Roman occupiers and to incite others to revolution. Theologically, Zealots were all but identical to the Pharisees, except for their fanatical, anti-Roman militancy. This view not only brought them into conflict with the Roman-friendly Sadducees, but it provoked Roman aggression against Jews.

The Sadducees differed significantly from Pharisees in their theology. They did not believe in a literal afterlife or a bodily resurrection. In fact, the Sadducees' primary interest was politics, which made them useful conduits for Roman power. They saw the Old Testament law in a less rigid light than the Pharisees, although committed to its core concepts. Of the four major sects of Judaism, the Sadducees were by far the most cooperative with Rome. They tended to be aristocrats and in control of the high priesthood.

Caiaphas and his father-in-law Annas were Sadducees. Because of their close but informal relationship with Pontius Pilate, what these men and their associates feared most was civil unrest among the Jewish commoners. Politically, such turmoil would reflect badly on Pilate. If Pilate lost his governorship, the Sadducees would lose their close and profitable partnership with the governor. Therefore, their relationship with Pilate had to be protected.

THE SANHEDRIN

The Sanhedrin was the supreme council, or court, in Israel during the life of Jesus. It was comprised of 70 men—largely Sadducees—plus the high priest (Caiaphas), who served as its president. Members of the Sanhedrin came from the chief priests, aristocrats, and scribes.

When Pontius Pilate was governor, the Sanhedrin had jurisdiction only over the province of Judea. The Sanhedrin had its own small police/guard detail that could arrest people who sought to disobey Temple rules or illegally enter its forbidden sections. While the Sanhedrin heard both civil and criminal cases and could technically assign a death penalty, it did not have the authority to execute a convicted criminal. Only Pontius Pilate had that authority.

Jewish Cultural Practices in the Time of Jesus: The Education of the Young

Life expectancy during the 1st Century was much lower than it is today. Men who lived past the age of 30-35 were considered the elders of their day. Women were expected to marry or get betrothed (with parental permission) after their 12th birthday plus one day. A female's expected life pursuit was marriage and motherhood; women received no formal education.

Jewish males began intensive study at a young age, but education for most concluded by age 15. For those bright or wealthy enough, higher education consisted of studying under a local rabbi, and if men distinguished themselves, they could begin teaching at the age of 30. If they didn't find a rabbi who accepted them as a student, then they entered the workforce by their mid-to-late teens.

The Apostles, already working at their trades, seem to have been rejected for formal education by other rabbis when Jesus hand-picked them as His pupils or disciples. A young Jewish male had a mindset of continuing his education at all costs. In light of this, the Apostles most likely began their journey with Jesus as teens or men in their early 20s.

Sacrificial Animals as Practiced by Judaism:

Of particular interest here is the Jewish practice of animal/blood sacrifice. According to William W. Hallo, Ph.D. and former Yale professor (see the November/December 2011 issue of *Biblical Archaeology Review*), the practice of animal sacrifice goes back to a Mesopotamian civilization called the Kushites [Cushites]. "The Kushites were Nilo-Saharans. Genesis 10 tells us that Nimrod, the son of Kush [Cush], moved into the Tigris-Euphrates Valley [from Egypt] and established a kingdom there. He brought with him the practice of the sacrifice of rams, bulls, and sheep. Abraham is a descendant of Nimrod. . . The sacrifice of animals was performed by priests and the oldest known caste of priests is that of the Horites who can be traced back to Nekhen in the Sudan (4000-3000 BC)."

The people of modern-day Israel share the same language and culture, shaped by their Jewish heritage and religion passed down through generations, starting with the founding father Abraham (ca. 1800 BCE). According to Leviticus (17:11), the purpose of animal sacrifice was for atonement, a personal reparation with God for a wrong or injury done to others—"because it is blood, as the seat of life, that makes atonement." According to Mosaic tradition, a blood sacrifice was considered a visible sign to God and all the community that underscored the sincerity of one's request for forgiveness of personal sin.

The sacrificial animal, which was typically a lamb or goat was necessarily a male according to Mosaic law, one year old, and without blemish. Each family or tribe was to offer one animal together. It was obligatory to determine who was to take part in the sacrifice so that the killing might take place with the proper intentions. . . The animal was slain on the eve of the Passover, on the afternoon of the 14th of Abib, after the Tamid sacrifice had been killed, i.e., at 3 PM.

When it came time for Moses and the Israelites to leave Egypt, God ordered that the blood of this sacrifice be painted on the doorposts of His people. This was to be a sign to the Lord, when passing through the land to slay the first-born of the Egyptians that night, that He should pass by the houses of the Israelites (Exodus 12:1-28). It was ordained, furthermore (Exodus 12:24-27), that this observance should be repeated annually for all time once the Israelites entered into their promised land (Exodus 12:25): "It will come to pass when you come to the land which the Lord will give you, just as He promised, that you shall keep this service."

Later, God spoke to Moses in the wilderness of Sinai on the first new moon of the second year following the exodus from the land of Egypt, saying: "Let the Israelite people offer the Passover sacrifice at its set time; you shall offer it on the fourteenth day of this month, at twilight, at its set time; you shall offer it in accordance with all its rites and rules." (*Num. 9:1–3, JPS translation*)

The Passover Sacrifice has since also come to be known as the Paschal Celebration or Feast in remembrance of how God saved the Israelites from death by having them mark their front doors with the blood of a sacrificial animal. That same night Moses led his people out of Egypt toward the Red Sea, which they later crossed to freedom in the desert and then on to Mt. Sinai.

THE JEWISH PRACTICE OF RITUAL IMMERSION

The baptism practiced by John the Baptist (see Chapter One) was an adaptation of the *mikvah,* or ritual immersion bath, that had been part of Jewish life for generations and symbolized a spiritual cleansing. It was part of the preparation for undertaking a new beginning. Jewish men took a *mikvah* each Sabbath in preparation for the new week. Women took a *mikvah* after each monthly period as a spiritual cleansing. On Yom Kippur the High Priest took *mikvot* (plural of *mikvah*) during the ceremonies in preparation for entering the Holy of Holies. Jesus came to John for a *mikvah* at the beginning of His ministry (Chapter One).

The reason John had people take a *mikvah* was to show that they had changed their minds and repented regarding their need for a Savior—more specifically that they were committing to taking a new direction regarding their salvation. No longer would they focus on keeping the Law but would look instead to the coming Redeemer whose arrival John the Baptist was announcing.

CHAPTER ONE

JERUSALEM
SPRING
29 AD

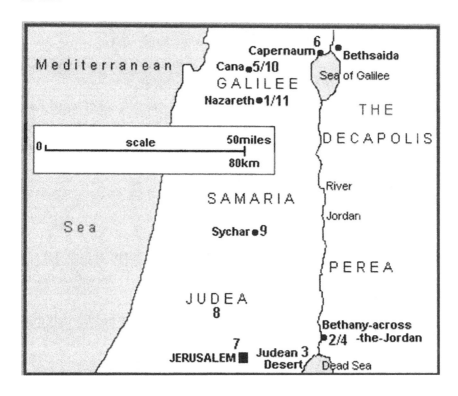

𝔍 ohn ben Abijah had reason to believe that the Holy Men of the Temple knew about his background and where had he come from and who had raised him. He believed that these Temple men had all the facts of what had happened to his parents and why he chose his unusual attire that began when, as a child, he had lived with the Essenes. Some of the Jewish elders thought that John had long ago separated himself from that controversial faction and exiled himself to the Judean Desert, where his preferred diet of locusts and wild honey existed in great abundance, thus fully enabling his chosen life of uninterrupted prayer.

The fact that Essene people had also long ago separated themselves from the usual Temple groups was no secret. In those days, the practicing Jews of Jerusalem considered the Essenes a strange and difficult group because of their dedication to asceticism, celibacy, voluntary poverty, and daily immersion. What these Temple men of Jerusalem didn't understand was that to John ben Abijah, the Essene people represented home—something he'd lost with the death of his parents at the hands of Herod, King of Judea.

As John grew older, his desire to learn the details of what had happened to his parents became a driving force. Taking note of the boy's obvious distress, some of the Essene elders took him aside one day and explained what they knew. They told him that when King Herod learned from the Magi of the birth of the long awaited Jewish Messiah and Savior of the Jewish people, foretold in scripture and by the prophets, Herod decided to kill all infants of two years or less. Shortly thereafter, Herod learned of the infant John's unusual birth circumstances; nonetheless, the King ordered the baby John killed.

But John's mother heard of Herod's intent and hid herself and her baby in the wilderness hills outside Jerusalem. The Royal assassins searched everywhere for the baby born to the aged couple Zechariah and Elizabeth. When she spotted her pursuers approaching her hiding place, she prayed to God for safety and the hill opened and concealed the mother and child. Shortly thereafter, as Zechariah, a Levi priest, was serving in the Temple, the King's

2

soldiers tried to learn from him the whereabouts of his wife and son. Refusing to betray his family, the soldiers murdered Zechariah; Elizabeth died of a broken heart forty days later.

The Essene elders finished telling John his family history by saying, "When we heard what had happened to your parents and that you had been left to die beside your mother, hidden in the countryside, all the elders of our sect met. We voted to take you into our family and raise you as if you were one of our own, and we're glad we did."

Tears had already welled up in young John's eyes, and out of gratitude he hugged the men who had told him of his family and how he came to live among them. Hugging was something John had learned from watching how the Essene women treated each other and their children—the men seldom hugged. As he hugged these men, he realized how happy it made him feel. "I'm glad too," the boy whispered to them wiping his eyes. "I hope one day to make all of you proud that you decided to take me in. Thank you for telling me the truth."

One day in the spring of 29 AD, John—now a grown man—showed up in the Jerusalem market, sitting and staring at the sky. He had long, thick hair like a lion's mane and wrapped himself in a camel's pelt that covered only one shoulder but reached to his knees. John sat in silence gazing at the sky for that whole week. On the eighth day, he moved to the Temple and began lecturing the Pharisees and Sadducees in his deep, commanding voice. Day in and day out, he announced to all who would listen that their only hope of salvation was to repent their sinful ways and request a water immersion which would cleanse their whole being with water.

And then, mere days later, John disappeared from the streets of the city.

———◆❊◆———

CAPERNAUM (*50 MILES NORTH OF BETHANY*)
SPRING
29 AD

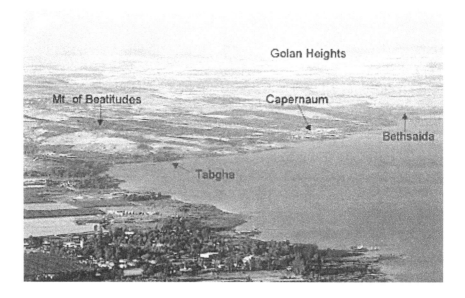

Word soon reached Jerusalem that John ben Abijah had actually relocated to the banks of the Jordan, where he continued his call for repentance and purification. Those who stood in the long queues in the surrounding area of Bethany were mostly from the families of fishermen, peddlers, or farmers. They came from the green pastures of Jericho, Bethel, and Galilee. Still others came from Judea and the surrounding regions of the Jordan and the fish-laden waters of Tabgha, Bethsaida, and Capernaum.

Andrew ben Jona belonged to such a family.

Fifteen-year-old Andrew lived in Capernaum with his father, older brother Simon and his wife, and their children, together with Simon's mother-in-law. The Jona family had always been fishermen; Simon owned his own fishing boat and often partnered with the Zebedee family. When word of the ongoing baptisms in the

Jordan reached Capernaum, several local families decided to make the journey to see for themselves if this man called John was the long-awaited Messiah and Savior. Andrew decided he wanted to go as well, and several of the families welcomed the young man into their pilgrimage train.

Acting with such conviction was unusual for Andrew. Although taller than most his age, he generally liked to keep to himself, do his work, and observe without being noticed. When he spoke, he usually had something worthwhile to say, but seldom felt comfortable being the first to say or do anything. The night before his scheduled departure for Bethany, his older brother Simon motioned for Andrew to meet in the woods nearby.

When they were finally alone, his brother leaned in close. "What are you doing?" Simon said through clenched teeth. Simon stood noticeably shorter than Andrew, though much thicker and more muscular with a full salt-and-pepper beard, and heavy eyebrows. Andrew had noticed his brother's bushy dark hair was beginning to recede. "Running off and leaving me and Dad to do your work. That's so unlike you!"

"I'm not 'running off,'" Andrew protested. "I asked Dad and he gave permission."

"Of course he gave you permission! You're the youngest! He always spoils you rotten! Maybe you can't see it, or maybe you just don't care, but Dad isn't getting any younger. He can barely keep up as it is! With you gone he'll work himself sick! Can't you see you're leaving too much for us to handle? We need you here!"

Andrew took a deep breath and put an arm around Simon's shoulders. "I already spoke with James and John. They told me they plan to go out with you and Dad in their own boat. If you need help, they promised to send some of their crew."

"That's not the point!" Simon said, red-faced and waving his arms.

"What *is* your point?"

"I know exactly why you want to go see this John the Baptizer. You're still trying to find a teacher to complete your education. But it's a fool's dream. Everyone your age will be going for the same reason. Why should he pick you? You're not special. You're nobody—a fisherman's son who lives 50 miles north! How could you possibly help a Master who's trying to start a congregation in Bethany?"

"I don't know," said Andrew. "I do live far away, but maybe that makes a strong point—that I've traveled so far to see him. It would certainly show that I'm serious about furthering my education. That I am dedicated." He thought for a moment. "And maybe John the Baptizer is the Messiah."

Simon shook his head. "You're such a child. Is this how it's going to be for the next three years? Every time somebody new says he's the Messiah, are you going to drop what you're doing and go see if he'll take you as one of his disciples?"

Andrew stared at Simon. "Insult me if you must. Call me a child or selfish or whatever you like. You're my older brother, and I love you. But I'm still going to Bethany in the morning."

BETHANY BEYOND THE JORDAN
SPRING
29 AD

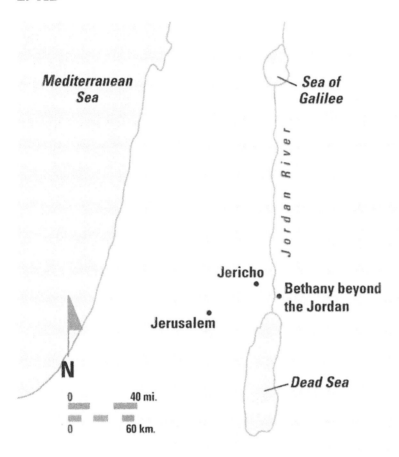

The immersion John now spoke of in Bethany was an adaptation of the *mikvah,* or ritual bath that had been part of Jewish life for centuries and symbolized a spiritual cleansing. It was part of the preparation for a new beginning. Jewish men took a *mikvah* each Sabbath in preparation for the new week. Women took a *mikvah* after each monthly period as a spiritual cleansing.

Some of the Holy Men of the Temple thought John to be

someone from a previous time come back to life. They sent young priests as emissaries to the Jordan with expensive gifts for the tall and bedraggled-looking man who stood all day in the river, baptizing those who asked for God's cleansing. John ignored the young Temple men dressed in their fine white linen robes, standing along the banks of the river trying to impress those who saw them.

But one day John couldn't help himself.

With long powerful legs, he pushed out of the river and up onto its steep embankment where the young priests stood, trying to attract his attention. Immediately, they fell to their knees. One of them placed gifts of oil and balm on the ground and respectfully pushed them toward him as he approached.

Seeing their offerings, he bristled. "What do you think you're doing?" he said, his deep voice echoing off the surrounding caves and back onto the slow moving Jordan. The murmurs of the crowd quieted.

"You are Elijah," one of the operatives said. "We bring you gifts of respect."

"I am not Elijah," he said plainly. "Our Father took him to heaven 900 years ago."

Silence filled the air while those in the long queues as well as John's disciples listened. "Are you the Messiah?" one of the young Temple men finally asked in a loud, obvious voice.

So that was their game. Their masters had sent them here to expose him as a false prophet.

"I am not the Messiah," John answered loudly, turning his back to the emissaries and putting his feet back into the water. "I am only a voice crying out in the wilderness; a voice saying to you, and to all, 'Follow the path of God and make firm His way.'"

His words echoed in all directions.

"Are you the prophet according to Moses?" another asked.

"No."

"Then tell us who you are!" They were clearly becoming frustrated. "If you are not the prophet or the Messiah, then by what authority do you baptize?"

"I am John, son of Zechariah and Elizabeth of Hebron who were murdered by King Herod. And I have no authority. I baptize in the name of our Father in heaven who will soon send a man whose sandals I am not fit to untie."

Having said this, he waded back into the calm, hushed river with its gentle stir of willow braids and locust leaves rhythmically lapping against the sheer, rocky banks.

Except for the Temple men, this same scene had played itself out beside the Jordan day after day. And the crowds continued to grow, despite the constant presence of the men in white. But John—always intense and focused upon whatever task was at hand—tirelessly baptized those who sought to be cleansed.

"Who is this Baptizer man?" one of the Temple men asked loudly, addressing the crowds. "Is he another prophet?"

John ignored him and motioned to the next person in line.

"Why won't he even answer a simple question?" the young Temple man barked, looking to see if any in the long lines had noticed this verbal assault. But no one cared. Their false flattery was an obvious trick.

The next person to wade toward John was a tall muscular male in his middle teens. "What is your name?" John asked.

"My name is Andrew."

"Where are you from?"

"I'm a fisherman from Capernaum."

"That's quite a long way you've traveled, Andrew from Capernaum. Do you wish to repent?"

"Yes. I want to be cleansed of youthful selfishness toward my fishing partners and family—especially my older brother."

The Baptizer nodded with quiet understanding and placed both hands on the teen's shoulders.

"Father in Heaven, hear our prayers of forgiveness and awakening for Andrew."

He then lowered the young fisherman into the Jordan back-first, one arm supporting the boy's broad back, while John's opposite hand pushed down on Andrew's forehead. John held him down for a few seconds and then pulled him up.

Andrew breathed deep and wiped the water from his eyes, staring at John.

Seeing that Andrew had quickly regained his composure, John lowered the young man back into the water again and said, "Let purity flow into Andrew and fill his entire being." After a few moments, he pulled the boy up.

Andrew smiled, eyes wide, but said nothing.

Once again, John lowered the youth. "We seal his repentance with this water of baptism, and may the fruits of his labor bring honor and glory to his loving Father in Heaven." With that, he brought Andrew up out of the water, the boy's face glowing.

"May I become one of your students?" Andrew asked in a hushed tone.

John stared at him for a moment. "If that is your wish."

CAPERNAUM
SPRING
29 AD

Young Andrew couldn't wait to tell family and friends. He borrowed a young donkey from one of the families he'd caravanned down to Bethany with and covered the 50 miles home in less than 12 hours. It was late afternoon when he arrived.

Andrew knew Simon and his Zebedee family partners would be at the docks mending nets and taking in supplies before going out for the night. After dark was the only time fishermen on the Sea of Galilee could successfully use their nets. Otherwise the tilapia, carp, and catfish would spot their nets and swim around them.

As Andrew jogged in the direction of the docks, he recognized his teenage friend John bar Zebedee ahead. The boy was one year younger and a little shorter in height than Andrew, but plucky, strong, and full of mischief. They usually made each other laugh, much to the annoyance of their elders.

Andrew ran up behind John, snickering as he came within ear shot. His friend strained and staggered under a load of fresh food and supplies, balancing it precariously on his broad shoulders. "Looks like you have everything *completely* under control there, good friend!"

"You *could* help, you know."

"Why? I'm having too much fun watching."

His friend burst out laughing. Still snickering, Andrew tried to steady his friend's load, but John was already shaking with laughter and the whole load of food and supplies crashed down onto the wooden dock. Both young men fell to their knees, laughing at the top of their lungs.

Moments later Simon and James bar Zebedee approached, obviously annoyed at the two teenagers. James was a big, strong young man in his late teens, almost as tall as Andrew, but as thick through his upper body and shoulders as Simon. John's older brother had a neatly trimmed beard and shoulder-length brown hair. "What in the world is going on with you two?" he grumbled. "There's nothing funny about spilling all our supplies and food. Look at the mess you idiots have made!"

"Oh, calm down," said John, beginning to pick up. "No one

asked you to be our parents. We'll clean it all up in no time without requiring any help from you."

"It's all my fault," said Andrew quietly. "I shouldn't have surprised him from behind. We'll have it on board before you know it."

"I thought you'd gone to Bethany," Simon said. "What are you doing back?"

"I have news to take your breath away," Andrew said, wide-eyed. "News that will change the course of history for our people!"

Simon and James exchanged a glance, shaking their heads.

"Look, Andrew," Simon said, "I know you mean well, but James and I have real work to do. Please hurry up with those supplies you managed to scatter so artfully all over the dock."

Without another word, Andrew and James turned and walked toward their boats.

"Don't listen to them. They take themselves entirely too seriously," said John, kneeling to begin gathering the family's fishing supplies. "Tell me this exciting news of yours."

BETHANY BEYOND THE JORDAN
SPRING
29 AD
SEVERAL DAYS LATER

When the Baptizer saw Andrew had brought his friend John to the banks of the Jordan, he welcomed both with open arms. And because Andrew had asked to become a disciple, the Baptizer gladly granted the heartfelt request of his friend to be baptized and join the ranks of his disciples. Since they were the newest, they were assigned the hardest and most thankless task—standing in the hot sun and managing the many long queues, making sure no one cut ahead of the others.

Thankfully, their years of fishing and the constant physical labor that entailed had in many ways prepared them for this. The searing heat, chattering families, and noisy animals felt very much like an average working day for the two friends from Capernaum.

Eventually, veteran disciples to the Baptizer noticed the responsible behavior of the two teenagers and instructed them to break for lunch and rest inside a cool cave where they could wash off the sweat and dust and refresh themselves. Andrew was satisfied with the fact that they would have to pay their dues and wait their turn for the Baptizer to begin teaching them, but he could tell that his friend was less patient.

Finally Andrew said, "What's bothering you?"

"Nothing," John muttered.

"Oh come on. I know you. And you're doing that quiet seething thing you always do when something's bothering you."

John sighed. "When do our instructions begin? He accepted us to be his disciples, but when does the teaching begin? I have no interest in standing out in the hot sun, directing unruly crowds, for the rest of my youth. We traveled pretty far to be here and for what? For this? I'd much rather be wasting my time on a boat mending nets or loading fresh supplies—at least I would know what I was doing!"

"Why are you always in such a hurry? Look, the Baptizer knows what he's doing. And we've only just arrived. We just have to pay our dues. Like with everything else."

Just then, the Baptizer walked into the cave. "I'll tell you why I'm not going to start teaching you now, my brothers," said the tall disheveled man. Andrew's face flushed with heat at the thought that the Baptizer had overheard his friend's doubts.

The baptizer took a skin of water and drank deep before raising his eyebrows at Andrew and John. "It's because I'm not the one you seek. The one you want is walking toward us right now. He's been waiting in line. Come see for yourself.”

With that, the Baptizer turned and walked out of the stone en-closure. John and Andrew raced to follow.

To Andrew’s eyes, the scene by the Jordan remained the same—the endless queues still snaked across the banks and cliffs in all directions as searing heat blazed down amidst the high pitch of men and women praying, blatting animals, barking dogs, cry-ing babies, and the incessant cacophony of flies, birds, and young Temple priests in white, still pretending to be men of importance.

The Baptizer proceeded directly into the water where a man of his approximate height waited on the bank. He had shoulder-length hair with a well-trimmed short beard to match and compassionate brown eyes that seemed to momentarily hypnotize the Baptizer.

“I know who you are,” the Baptizer finally said. The two men studied each other, as though they had met before. “Why have you come?”

“I’ve come to be baptized,” said the stranger.

“But why?” said the Baptizer. “It is you who should baptize me.”

“I’m asking you to, please, baptize me,” insisted the wide-eyed, handsome stranger. “It is how it is meant to be. I don’t ask for my-self, but on behalf of my Father.”

Hearing those words, the Baptizer took the man by the hand and led him into the Jordan. “As you request. I ask you, do you wish to be baptized?”

“Yes.”

The Baptizer nodded and took hold of the man, as he had the others before Him.

Suddenly the sky darkened and a light breeze pushed aside the blazing heat. “Father in Heaven,” the Baptizer said, “hear our prayers for this man whose sandals I am not fit to untie.” He then lowered the man into the Jordan back-first, one arm support-ing his broad back, while his opposite hand pushed down on his forehead. He held the stranger under for a few seconds and then pulled him up.

The man wiped the water from his eyes, staring back at the Baptizer and quietly speaking to the Baptizer with words not even Andrew could make out from mere meters away.

Seeing that he had regained his composure, the Baptizer lowered the man back into the water again and said, "We seal this man with the blessed waters of the Jordan, and may the fruits of His labor be wholly according His loving Father in Heaven."

The Baptizer brought the man up out of the water once more and Andrew and John gasped, speechless.

The man's body appeared to glow with white light, as if a sun had entered His being. The dark clouds above opened, and a ball of light appeared and descended, coming to rest on the stranger's wet shoulders.

Andrew squinted—the light... it had wings! Like the bird after Noah's flood!

A Voice, from nowhere and everywhere all at once, broke the silence that had fallen over the throngs of people on the shore.

"THIS IS MY BELOVED SON, WITH WHOM I AM WELL PLEASED."

The sky blackened and a vicious dust devil swirled, spraying sand, pebbles, and water at those close by. People fell to the ground to protect themselves and their loved ones. The two friends from Capernaum did the same.

Then, in the blink of an eye, the sky cleared, the wind stopped, the sun came out, and the stranger was nowhere to be seen.

Andrew ran across the water to the Baptizer. "Where did He go?"

"Don't worry," the older man said, smiling. "He told me He wants to talk to you and your friend. He's withdrawn to a quiet place to pray. He's the one you've really been looking for."

"When can we meet Him?" John asked.

The Baptizer looked them both in the eye as though examining them. "You'll meet Him when He's ready."

The two teenagers looked at each other and shrugged. "I guess we'll just get back to helping with the lines then?" Andrew said.

John nodded.

Andrew and John arose at dawn the next day, and as they left their cave, the Baptizer awaited them.

"Sleep well?"

Andrew looked at John, then back at the Baptizer. "Yes, fine, thanks. Just..."

"What is it?" the Baptizer asked.

"What happened yesterday—did it really happen?"

"Did your eyes see it happen?"

"Yes," Andrew replied.

"Did our Father in heaven give you your eyes?"

"Yes," Andrew said again.

"Then do not doubt."

John and Andrew exchanged another look.

"But did you mean it?" Andrew pressed.

"Mean what?"

John spoke up. "You said that man was the one we've been looking for."

"Aren't you looking for the Messiah? The Lamb of God?" the Baptizer asked.

"Yes," said John, "but aren't you the one?"

"No." The Baptizer smiled at the boys and directed their attention across the river.

The tall stranger from yesterday walked into view on the opposite bank of the river and began washing His face. "That man is the one you seek," the Baptizer said, pointing. "He is the Lamb of God."

16

Andrew and John looked at each other, frowning. "Really?" they chorused.

The Baptizer smiled. "Really. *He* is the Son of God!"

The two friends ran as fast as they could across a shallow part of the river, splashing and yelling at the top of their lungs for the tall man to stop and wait.

The man stopped and waited for the two to catch up. As they came up to Him, He said, "Why are you shouting? What's the matter?"

Andrew and John stopped short, out of breath and puzzled. They shrugged their shoulders and kicked at the ground, unsure of what to say. "We're wanting to talk to you," Andrew finally said. "Maybe we could go with you to where you're going. The Baptizer said you were the one we were looking for."

"What does that mean?" asked the man.

"It means," John said, "that we think you're the Messiah of our people, and someone we would like to spend our days and nights learning from—a blessed Rabbi, the Lamb of God."

The tall man studied the two teenagers, nodding in thought. "Come with me, and we can talk about this in private." He turned and began to walk ahead.

They turned a corner and Andrew tapped John's shoulder as two familiar faces approached. James and Simon ran toward them, out of breath. Andrew and John stared in disbelief at the sudden appearance of their older brothers.

"What's the matter, brother?" John said.

"What are you doing?" James gasped. "Are you going to follow that stranger?"

"What are you doing here?" Andrew said to Simon. "When last we spoke, you told me I was acting the fool. Why have you come here—to save us from our own stupidity?"

"It's not like that, dear brother," Simon said. "You know my mother-in-law is sick. But she had a dream. She said I needed to find you and the man you were going to follow. She believes He could cure her, so we came looking for you."

"How did you find us?" John asked.

"Who could miss you?" said James. "That spectacle you two made running across the Jordan, yelling and screaming at the top of your lungs. You looked like crazed idiots!"

"Well, maybe we are," said John.

"According to the Baptizer," Andrew said, "*that man* is the Messiah we've been waiting for these many years. And He's invited us to follow Him to a place where we can talk."

"Can we come too?" asked Simon.

"That depends," said John. "Do you still think we're 'crazed idiots?'"

"No," said Simon with kindness in his voice. "We don't think you're crazy, just a little impetuous, which makes us worry about your doing something foolish. But in this case, much as it pains me to admit it, it appears you two have been the wiser, and we're the ones who need to listen."

Simon looked up ahead and saw that the tall stranger had stopped and was waving for all four to follow. They moved forward again as the man turned a corner.

James twisted his mouth and sighed as they raced to catch up. "Look, we're really sorry we were rude to you both. Please forgive us. But I do think it's time all of us get to know this Messiah of yours. What's His name, anyway?"

They turned the corner and nearly ran headfirst into the tall stranger.

"I am Jesus, of Nazareth."

18

CHAPTER TWO

JERUSALEM
DAWN, THE FIRST DAY
FRIDAY, APRIL 3, 33 AD

Seventeen year old John bar Zebedee fought tears as he raced through the streets of Jerusalem with news of how the High Priests and Sanhedrin had organized a trial in the middle of the night against Jesus. Dawn peered over the horizon when John finally stumbled to the top of the stairs to the Upper Room where a sleep-deprived Mother Mary and seven of her female friends sobbed and paced the floor. They already knew that Jesus had been arrested the night before by the Jewish leaders because of Judas and his treachery.

Gasping, the boy bent over to catch his breath and blurted for all the women to hear, "They mean to have Jesus crucified."

Mother Mary placed both hands over her ears, collapsed to the floor, and wailed.

Mary Clopas, her sister visiting from Emmaus, and Mary Magdalene hurried to her side.

John caught his breath and wiped his face on a sleeve. "I've been watching the trial. They're taking him to see Pilate now. For sentencing."

Mother Mary quieted as under the weight of the dread that swept through the room.

"How can they have a secret trial in the middle of the night?" blurted Mary Clopas. "It's against the law!"

"They will find a loophole," Mary Magdalene stated quietly. "They will lie for each other and say it was, by the letter, done according to the Law." The others looked at her, candles flickering in an early morning breeze. "The truth will be whatever they say it is."

"We have to go see what Pilate's going to do with Him," Mother Mary said, her voice cracking. "The governor is our only hope."

"You're right," Magdalene said, bowing her head in a moment of silent prayer. "The High Priests cannot order His death; only Pilate can. If he can see that they're setting him up to take all the blame for the recent unrest in the eyes of Rome, we might have a chance.

"What happened to Simon—no—Peter?" Mary Clopas said, stumbling over his new name.

John shrugged. "They invited him to watch, but he ran away."

"Then we better get going," Mother Mary said, wiping tears and sweat from her ashen face. "He has to know He's not alone. He has to know that I love Him. My Son..."

"I pray we're not too late," John said, leading the way and running down the stairs. "Follow me and hurry!"

JERUSALEM
GOLGOTHA, THE FIRST DAY
FRIDAY, APRIL 3, 33 AD
APPROXIMATELY 3:00 P.M.

Once Roman Commander Longinus and his men shoulder-dragged the bloody and limp Nazarene up the steep Golgotha terrain the centurion ordered the area sealed from atop his large, imposing black horse. Dressed in battle gear for crowd control,

Longinus' soldiers assumed an oval formation around the peak of the stony mesa. No crazed Jewish zealots were going disturb a Longinus-directed execution.

He allowed only young John to escort the sweaty and blood-splattered mother of Jesus and her two female friends to the foot of the cross, believing the boy to be the mother's youngest son. "Do what you have to do," Pilate had ordered him, "but remember I didn't want to kill this man. A little compassion for the family might help people see that."

Young John was not surprised that Mother Mary could bare-ly stand when she first arrived at the crucifixion site about three hours ago. He still didn't really know what he should do to help; there were no adults he could turn to. Older brother James, along with Peter, Andrew, and the others, had fled into hiding from the Roman soldiers who had been dispatched throughout the city by Pilate to arrest any followers of Jesus.

Somehow Mother Mary had found the strength to wrap her arms around the blood-streaked cross, and Mary Clopas and Mary Magdalene wrapped arms around their friend to lend support—and prevent her collapse.

Thick, dark clouds over the city roiled into one another, horizon to horizon. A stiff swirling breeze began to dry the blood still flow-ing from Jesus' wounds. Looking up the cross, John thought He appeared ready to die. This was really happening. And there was nothing he or anyone else could do to stop it.

Jesus coughed, squinting open one swollen bloody eye, gazing down at His mother. "Woman," He whispered, "behold your son." Then, shifting His gaze to John, He said, "Behold your mother." He sighed and closed both eyes.

Centurion Longinus, seeing that the two men being crucified alongside the Nazarene were still alive, commanded that his men stop what they were doing and break the legs of the other two with sledge hammers. Without support from their legs, the two criminals would immediately die of suffocation. But he could see that the Nazarene was about to die.

Jesus cleared His throat. "I thirst," He said in a loud whisper.

Longinus commanded his men to soak a sponge in a nearby barrel of common brine, mount it on a lance, and push it up to where Jesus could place His mouth around it.

Jesus opened one eye and sucked on the brine-filled sponge, quickly letting it fall from His mouth. A few minutes passed and His gasping grew more ragged and labored. At last He said, "It is finished."

His head fell forward onto His gashed and bloody chest and He breathed no more.

John wrapped an arm around Mother Mary to keep her from falling.

She shouted up at her son, "Jesus, Jesus, my Son!"

At that moment, bolts of lightning flashed and re-flashed across the dark clouds, followed by numerous, deafening claps of thunder. The earth shook and groaned, knocking many of the soldiers to their knees. Powerful gusts of wind suddenly blasted across the hilltop.

Mother Mary and her female companions clung to the cross as the ground heaved and rumbled. "I've lost my Son!" the Mother of Jesus whispered through tears.

Her friends shrieked, clutching each other while easing themselves to the ground to keep from being tossed down the steep stone-covered embankment.

"Hurry up!" Longinus shouted to be heard by his men. The ground lurched again and the sky roared, air whipping in all directions. "Break those other men's legs!"

"What about the one in the middle?" asked one of his men,

shoving a long lance into the ground to keep his balance.

"No need!" Longinus shouted. He took the lance from the soldier's hand and rammed it into Jesus from His right side, upward into the chest and heart cavity. A stream of blood and water spurted out onto Longinus' face, and the rest ran down the body of Jesus onto the cross. The women holding to the base shrieked in horror. Longinus pulled a clean cloth from inside his sleeve and wiped his face, tossing the lance back to his soldier. "He's dead!"

"Look what you've done," Magdalene shouted at Longinus, still wiping his own face. Stretching her bloodied hands up at the centurion, she sobbed, "Did your mother teach you to be such a heartless cur?"

Longinus flung his blood-stained cloth to the ground. "You know nothing!" he replied.

A flash of lightning gave them all a quick glimpse of the blood-drenched corpse of Jesus. Ugly open wounds and lacerations seemed to have replaced the flesh of his arms, shoulders, chest, and legs—they could even see some of His exposed bone and tissue.

Tears ran down John's face as he fought the urge to vomit. He couldn't understand how Jesus had been able to carry His cross.

"My Son... my Son..." Mother Mary whimpered.

John placed an arm around her and tried to guide her away from the cross, but she broke away and collapsed onto her knees. She covered her eyes with both hands and screamed through sobs, "They've taken my Son! He's gone! My blessed Son is gone!"

Longinus and his men had been warned by Pilate and the chief priests that once Jesus died, they could expect almost anything from His followers, including a full-fledged suicide charge. Now that Jesus was dead, the Roman centurion, in the interests of safety, once again instructed his men to form a tight defense ring around the three crosses.

"Surely," Longinus said to himself. "This man was the Son of God."

But no gathering of Jesus' disciples materialized. Sunset would soon arrive and Jewish law required that everyone be removed from their crosses before then. The two men on crosses to either side of Jesus were gasping for breath, dying now that their legs had been broken. The thunder had quieted and there was a sad stillness to the air on Golgotha.

The squeaking of wooden wheels preceded the arrival of an elder gentleman accompanied by several workmen pulling a cart with ladders and other carpentry tools approaching the soldiers standing guard.

"Halt!" shouted Longinus from astride his huge horse. "State your name and purpose."

The old man and his party complied. John recognized the old man as someone who had argued in the Sanhedrin that Jesus should be treated fairly by the high court.

"My name is Nicodemus," the man shouted. "I'm a member of the Sanhedrin."

Longinus nodded knowingly. He recognized the decorated tunic, belt, overcoat, and headgear of a doctor of the Temple. "And why are you here?" the centurion said.

"I have come with my servants to assist with the burial of the Nazarene."

"And why would I require your help? I have more than enough men for the task."

"Because another member of the Sanhedrin is with your governor as we speak, obtaining written permission that we be allowed to give this crucified Jew an honorable burial before sunset, in accordance with the law."

"And who is this other member of the Sanhedrin?"

"Joseph of Arimathea. He and I both met with your governor, and he agreed to provide written permission. Joseph should be here any moment with a tablet containing said permission, along with the seal of his Excellency."

"If he isn't, you would leave me no alternative but remove the Nazarene and dump him in an open grave along with the others."

CHAPTER THREE

JERUSALEM
FIRST LIGHT, THE FIRST DAY
FRIDAY, APRIL 3, 33 AD

Roman census records showed that Jerusalem had a population of approximately 600,000 people before Passover. However, the Jewish leaders of the city expected that during the days surrounding this most important of Jewish feast days that the city's population would swell by at least another 250,000. Families visiting from out of town would double and triple up with each other and quickly fill available inn and guest lodging spaces, while latecomers would have to pitch endless rows of tents outside the city walls. According to tradition, Passover had already begun at sunset the previous day, a celebration which Jesus had shared with His Apostles.

At the next morning's early light, city residents and visitors began streaming into the streets. The scheduled activities of the day centered around the Temple, but there were other events taking place of which few were aware unless they happened to cast their eyes to the top of Golgotha.

Many of the people now navigating the streets between Passover activities had waved palm branches just a few days before and sung and shouted with joy as they watched Jesus ride into the city on a young donkey. These excited Judeans were convinced that their Jesus was the long-awaited Messiah—and that He would declare Himself during Passover.

They further believed that their Messiah would eventually lead His new revolutionary army to victory over the insidious tyranny of the Romans and reclaim Israel for God's people. They couldn't wait to be eye-witnesses to a new beginning for their nation. They and their ancestors had been praying for this moment for over 500 years.

At the peak of Golgotha, Roman centurion Longinus closely eyed Nicodemus and his servants, then nodded in their direction. Pilate had ordered Longinus to remove all three men from their crosses before sunset. This day was the day of Preparation, and the Jewish leaders had implored him to make sure the bodies of the three crucified men did not hang through the night. The next day was the Sabbath, and a very special one, because it was also Passover.

Longinus looked at John, still standing with the women. Tears had stained the boy's dust-covered face, and he appeared confused and paralyzed with grief. Mother Mary and her friends had been huddled and praying at the foot of the cross since the Nazarene had been nailed and raised on the wooden death structure.

But now, seeing that her son was truly gone, the Mother of the Nazarene laid down on her side sobbing. Her friends tried to get her to swallow some water, their own faces gaunt and wan from the horrors of the day. Lighting still flashed and danced across the dark sky, punctuated by an occasional thunder clap.

The centurion turned back to Nicodemus. "I believe you," Longinus said, carefully choosing his words. "Since I know from your garments that you *are* a member in good standing of the Sanhedrin, you might as well get started taking down the dead Nazarene. But your friend, Joseph, had best arrive quickly with that note from Pilate. There's little time before sunset. If you don't bury Him before then, He'll be thrown into the open burial pit and burned with the others."

Nicodemus studied Longinus a moment and nodded. "I thank you, centurion, from my heart," said the elderly Pharisee. "May God bless you for your generous courtesy. I promise, you will not be sorry."

The older man next removed his mantle and young John did the same. Nicodemus directed his servants to bring ladders to the cross where Jesus hung inert and dead, blood and water still oozing down His body.

Mother Mary, seeing what was taking place, pulled herself up into a sitting position with the assistance of her friends and leaned back against the foot of the cross.

John and Nicodemus steadied the ladders while the servants climbed towards the horizontal cross beam, carpentry levers and tongs in hand. Nicodemus instructed them on how to loosen the nails without fully removing them.

"We don't want Jesus to fall," he said.

"Thank you, Nicodemus," Mother Mary managed to whisper.

He smiled at her as best he could and instructed the workmen to wrap long cloth-covered leather straps around Jesus' chest and feet and loop the straps over the wooden cross beam in readiness to support the full weight of the corpse.

"What can I do?" asked John.

"Don't trouble yourself, boy," Nicodemus said. "We have this well in hand."

"Please," implored John. "I want to help."

Nicodemus regarded the boy a moment, then nodded. "Very well. Grab another ladder. When Joseph gets here, we're going to lower Him slowly to the ground."

"And into my lap, please," Mother Mary said barely above a whisper, shaking her head. "I need to look upon my Son's face one last time."

Nicodemus nodded that he understood her request and would do what she asked.

Another call and response of lightning and thunder lit up the sky and interrupted all speech.

Longinus, who had been silently watching the activity at the cross from the saddle of his big, shiny black horse, took notice of the sounds of an approaching horse. He turned and saw an older man in Sanhedrin robes on a white horse at the bottom of the hill looking up at the three crosses.

Joseph of Arimathea rode high in his saddle and slowly guided his beautiful Arabian steed up the steep Golgotha grade, the signed document from Pilate in one hand, while he observed all taking place above him. He was a tall, white-haired man in his late forties who clearly knew his way around horses. His look and carriage conveyed aristocracy and breeding. When he finally arrived where the soldiers stood guard, they directed him to Longinus.

A deep aftershock grumbled beneath the ground.

Without words, Joseph steadied his horse and handed the document to Longinus.

"Is this from the governor?" the centurion asked.

"It is."

"Are you Joseph of Arimathea?"

"I am."

"Thank you," Longinus said, opening and glancing over the document, ensuring the presence of Pilate's official seal. "You may proceed," he said over the din.

Joseph rode to the cross, dismounted, removed a long linen sheet from a saddle bag, and walked to where Mother Mary sat. "We'll need this, for when we lower Him to the ground."

"She wants Jesus lowered into her lap," Nicodemus said.

Mother Mary looked up at Joseph as he placed the long burial sheet across the woman's lap, her face puffy with exhaustion and soaked with tears. She extended both hands toward the white-haired gentleman. "Thank you, dear Joseph. And you, Nicodemus. Both of you are an answer to a mother's prayers." She took a deep breath. "And yes, please place my Son here as best you can," she said, pointing to her lap. "I need to say my last goodbye."

Joseph and Nicodemus then mounted other ladders and meticulously removed the nails from Jesus' hands, making sure to not enlarge the wounds. John, on a different ladder, was now able to absorb the weight of Jesus' torso by pulling tighter on the straps already wrapped around the wooden cross-beam and across the boy's shoulders. All that was left to do now was loosen and remove the long, thick nail that impaled both feet of Jesus.

The two older men asked John to pull the straps as tight as he could to relieve some of the pressure from Jesus' feet. Taking great care to not enlarge that wound required patience as both older men gently loosened the huge nail with the aid of levers, tongs, and a stone they found lying on the ground. It took several minutes, but finally they were able to completely remove the huge spike. Blood squirted from the wound, then went limp, onto their hands and down the cross.

Jesus' feet swung free and both men gave a sigh of relief while John held on as best he could to keep the body from falling. "Finally," Joseph said.

"A little help, please?" John pleaded.

Both men looked up and saw the overwhelming physical strain John was under supporting the full weight of the corpse. Quickly, they climbed to where they could place their hands beneath the body and give it support. Slowly, the three walked the body of Jesus down the ladders and lowered Him onto the lap of Mother Mary.

Longinus could see that he no longer had to concern himself with Jesus. The two older Sanhedrin men seemed to have things well in hand, but he still had to bury the two criminals.

"Thank you, my dear friends," Mother Mary said to John, Joseph, and Nicodemus, fighting tears. She looked upon her Son and her face trembled at the sight. He looked so tired. "Why did these men hate Him so? All He did was teach people to act with love."

The two Marys knelt beside Mother Mary, drying her face and offering water.

Gently, she pushed them aside, tears inching down her face. "It's always been so hard for us—He and I and my wonderful husband—to talk. So much has always been left unsaid and now—now it's too late. He's dead, and I should have said more! I should have told Him how much I love Him—how proud of Him I am."

She ran her fingers through his long, blood-caked hair. Her hand caught on the crown of thorns and a small trickle of blood seeped from her index finger. She winced in pain, then reached forward, pulling at the wreath of barbs with each hand.

A bolt of lightning spider-webbed across the sky and deafening thunder followed. The small party covered their ears, except Mary, who focused on removing the circle of thorns.

Joseph of Arimathea looked up at the roiling clouds. "We're going to have to hurry to get Him buried. We're running out of daylight."

"Of course, Joseph," Mary Magdalene said, rubbing Mother Mary's shoulder as she fiddled with the thorns. "But where? No one was prepared for this. We have no tomb!"

"I have a place," Joseph said. "It's nearby in a well-kept garden and never been used."

Mother Mary took a deep breath and slowly moved her head side-to-side. "Joseph, you are most kind, but I have no ability to pay for such a tomb."

Joseph bowed slightly. "You need not concern yourself with that. It's a gift. And our dear friend Nicodemus here has already left spices at the sepulcher. But as you can see," he said, looking up at the dark sky, flashing again with lightning, "It is Preparation Day. Please let's not waste anymore time."

John and the other women added short words of agreement.

"Mother Mary," Magdalene pleaded, "please. It's time."

The mother of Jesus bowed her head, exhausted and spent. "You're right," she whispered. Peering up at Joseph, she said, "Please remove Him from my lap."

Joseph and Nicodemus picked up both ends of the sheet on which Jesus lay. John rushed to help with one end and both of Mary's friends quickly joined Nicodemus. Underneath the sheet, all three men used their mantles to lend further support and began walking toward the close-by burial site with the assistance of two servants.

Mother Mary stood, following in their wake with the support of her friends. "Please be gentle, dearest friends," she whispered.

Sweat streamed down the faces of Joseph, Nicodemus, and the youthful Apostle John. They were walking as fast as they could toward the burial site, but were also very short of breath under the dead weight of Jesus. Another mild aftershock rumbled and grumbled beneath their feet, causing them to stumble along the sloping garden terrain. A flash lit up the sky, followed by another violent clap of thunder overhead.

The smell of newly bloomed flowers and fresh grass filled the nostrils of the burial procession. Tears still flowed down Mother Mary's cheeks as she staggered along. She was doing her best to keep up while her friends held her tight with the grim determination that she would not fall.

"Joseph, how much further?" Mary Magdalene finally asked.

"We're almost there," he answered.

"I certainly hope so," she whispered. "The night will be upon us soon."

Jesus' body needed to be washed, wrapped, and buried before sunset to satisfy the Law, and it all had to be accomplished before they could roll the large round stone into place and seal the sepulcher.

Chapter Four

℧ orah Law left nothing to chance concerning the burial of executed Jews:

> *"If a man has committed a sin worthy of death, and he is put to death, and you hang him on a tree, his corpse shall not hang all night on the tree, but you shall surely bury him on the same day, for he who is hanged is the curse of God, so that you do not defile your land which the Lord your God gives you as an inheritance." (Deuteronomy 21:22-23; cf. Joshua 8:29, 10:26-27).*

Joseph and Nicodemus left Mother Mary with young John in the garden outside the tomb, not only so he could comfort her as best he could, but to make sure she didn't come back into the tomb. These two respected members of the Sanhedrin, their servants, and the women worked hard at covering the body in the myrrh, aloe, and oil Nicodemus had sent ahead.

"Quickly, please, ladies," Joseph said.

"We're going as fast as we can," Mary Magdalene said. To fail to have all the burial preparations completed by sundown would be a sacrilege, which could mean punishment by death for all involved. "It'd be easier if we had more oil."

Another sudden outburst from Mother Mary outside echoed through the tomb.

"Or another set of hands," muttered Mary Clopas.

"There's no arguing with grief," Mary Magdalene said.

Outside, John patiently intercepted another charge from Mother Mary. "Mother," the boy pleaded, "they have to complete the preparations before dark! There's too much to do! Please understand!"

"I understand, John, but I need to see my Son. Who knows when I might see Him again?"

"You will see Him again, Mother, I promise," John insisted. "On Sunday we will all re-open the grave so as to properly complete His burial. Joseph and Nicodemus and the women will make sure of that. You can see your Jesus then."

Mother Mary took a deep breath and wiped her eyes, face still ashen. Looking up into the blackening sky, she whispered, "A lot can happen between now and then."

As the last light of the sky began fading to dark, everyone came out into the garden led by Joseph holding a torch high so all could see their way. "All is in order," he said. "More linens, spices, myrrh, and herbs are needed, but they can all be added after the Sabbath." Turning to Nicodemus, he said, "It's time to seal the tomb."

"No, no," Mother Mary pleaded. "I have to say good-bye to my Son."

"Not now, Mother" said John. "There isn't time."

"He's right," Joseph said. "We cannot delay any further."

Following detailed instructions from Joseph and Nicodemus, the servants moved to their assigned positions and began rolling the huge circular stone into place to prevent entrance or exit from the tomb. The stone, more than eight feet in diameter and twelve inches wide, weighed several hundreds of pounds and had been carefully set in position when the sepulcher had been built to Joseph's specifications months ago. Though the rough-surfaced wheel rested on a metal track, it was still no easy task for the servants to push the enormous wheel into place.

The women and John tried to restrain Mother Mary as the stone rotated along its path, but she finally pulled from their grasp, ran to the stonework, and threw herself against it, scraping her face and hands.

"Move the stone back!" she implored. "I need to see my Son!"

Joseph walked to her and handed her a clean cloth for the fresh abrasions.

"Mary, I'm afraid we cannot do that," he explained as gently as he could. "We've just barely met the requirements of the Law. To open the tomb now would be a desecration. A dangerous one. For all of us. You will be able to see your Son after the Sabbath, once we put the rest of His burial spices in place. I'm so very sorry."

Mary collapsed to the ground in front of the stone and sobbed, her body quaking with grief. Mary Clopas and Mary Magdalene rushed to her aid with more clean cloths and a small water skin.

From the encroaching darkness, three Roman guards marched into view, clanking their way toward the huge stone burial door. Thinking they might intend harm to Mother Mary, the remaining burial party huddled around the grief-stricken woman.

"What is the meaning of this, centurion," asked Joseph. "Why are you here?"

The soldiers stopped short, taking in the scene.

Mother Mary took no notice and continued sobbing.

"We're under orders from the governor," said a centurion. "We're to make sure no one opens this sealed tomb. We're to remain on post until relieved." The commander looked around at the others. "Who are all of you?" he asked. "What's going on?"

"We're family and friends of Jesus, the Nazarene," Joseph explained. "We've just finished burying Him, and are now preparing to return to our homes."

"Who's she?" the officer asked, pointing at Mother Mary.

"His Mother," said Nicodemus.

"Get her out of here," said the centurion. It wasn't a request. "Go home, and stay inside. It will not be safe in this city for any of you tonight."

Joseph nodded at the others that they should leave. "Thank you, centurion, for your kindness and concern for our safety. We appreciate your compassion for our grief."

Joseph reached down to help Mary Magdalene and Mary Clopas lift Mother Mary to her feet, but she swatted their hands away.

"Leave me alone!" she sobbed, wiping her face. "I'm not afraid of these soldiers. If I want to stay here, I will."

The Roman soldiers froze in place, poised for trouble.

Mary Magdalene saw the danger. "Mother, there is much that needs to be done, and only you can do it. But it needs to be done immediately at your home, this night."

"She's right," said Nicodemus.

"You can do the most good from home," Joseph added. "Your friends need you."

The apostle John knelt down beside her and spoke softly. "Mother, I need you to come with me now and come home. I don't know what these Roman soldiers are planning, but I need to take care of you just as your Son requested. Will you please come with me now, so I can do as He asked?"

She looked up and gazed deep into the boy's big brown eyes, tears and blood still flowing across her face. After a few moments, she looked away and stared up to the top of Golgotha where the flames of the other criminals' cremation danced and flickered. She wiped her face again, nodded, and turned back to the young apostle.

"Yes, John," she whispered absently, "I will go with you now. . . just as my dear Son asked."

━━━◆━━━

JERUSALEM
BEGINNING OF THE SABBATH (AT DARK)
33 AD
THE FIRST DAY

As highly respected members of the Sanhedrin, Joseph and Nicodemus were well known on sight throughout Jerusalem by many of its residents—Nicodemus was one of the wealthiest men in the city. And yet, these two esteemed gentlemen, their servants, the apostle John, Mother Mary, along with Mary Magdalene and Mary Clopas all hid their faces and took great pains to blend with the rest of the pedestrian foot traffic that evening as their small group made its way back through the city.

The warning by the Roman soldier weighed heavily in their thoughts. The tense journey passed slowly, with virtually no words spoken. There was too much to be said, but no one dared speak their mind out loud, lest they be overheard and brought to the attention of the Romans. Mary Magdalene had serious reservations about what the soldiers had really been instructed to do by their superiors. She suspected that the soldiers were more worried about the possibility of civil unrest than they were about the followers of Jesus—at least for the time being.

When they finally arrived back at The Cenacle, Mary of Zebedee, sisters Martha and Mary, as well as long-time disciples Susanna and Joanna greeted the four witnesses to the day's horrors with loving tears and hugs. They offered to help John with Mother Mary, but he waived them off. Mary Magdalene reminded the two elder gentlemen that the Mother of Jesus wanted any articles of memorabilia that had touched her Son that day—anything they could find would be greatly appreciated. Both men promised to return sometime on Sunday so as to help everyone complete the burial protocols for Jesus along with any desired keepsakes they could locate from that horrible Friday.

John slowly escorted Mother Mary into the bedroom and lowered her onto her bed. She sighed and wearily laid back, rolling to one side and assuming a fetal position. When a few moments had passed, she said, "John, tomorrow when it's first light, would you please go back to Golgotha and see if you can find any of my Son's things—the clothes He was wearing, the lance, the crown of thorns—I think I dropped it—anything . . . you know what I mean?"

"Yes, Mother, I understand."

"Anything you could find would mean a great deal to me."

"Yes, I understand. The others will be looking as well."

Mother Mary nodded and became silent. After a minute, she whispered, "Please leave me. I need to pray for my Son and tell Him how much I love Him. And I need to pray for the Apostles—especially Judas."

John gently placed a blanket on his new Mother and carefully closed her door behind him. His head throbbed from lack of sleep and his arms and legs ached from overuse. He'd had no sleep since the night before last, and it was all catching up with him. He'd watched God-made-man mercilessly tortured and murdered, then had to help bury Him. He forced himself to keep his broken-heartedness to himself. There were enough people crying—his tears would serve no purpose.

He turned from Mary's door and saw a small crowd of Jesus' disciples and friends kneeling in prayer throughout the room. He noticed the front door had been double-locked.

"Mother Mary wishes to be alone," he announced quietly, "so

she can pray."

Mary Magdalene came to the boy and gave him a firm embrace. "John, you're bringing great comfort to our Mother," she said in a soft voice. "We're all so proud of you and how strong you've been this terrible day. Thank you for making yourself available for Jesus and the rest of us. I don't know what we would have done without you."

She pulled a cloth from her pocket and began to dry his face.

John shook his head and covered his face. "I should have done more," he said, falling to his knees, fighting tears. "I should have done more . . ." He covered his face with both arms and prostrated himself on the floor.

Magdalene knelt and placed a hand on his head, sighing. "We all should have, John. I know I wish I had. But who knows? Maybe it wouldn't have changed a thing? Remember, He warned us many times. We just never thought it would be like... like this."

Mary Clopas joined them. "You've done just fine, John," she added. "We've all been trying to do our best, but none of us really know what to do . . . from the moment we ran out of here this morning. If it hadn't been for you, we may never have known what happened. The burial may not have happened. He could have been cremated."

A loud knocking on the front door interrupted all conversation.

John slowly rose, wiping his eyes. "Quick everyone, hide," he whispered. "Someone may have recognized us when we walked back from the garden."

He walked apprehensively to the front door, thanking God in his head for it being double-locked. "Who is it?" he said, standing to one side of the door.

"My name is Veronica," came a hoarse and weary voice. "and I have a gift for the Mother of Jesus."

"Are you by yourself?" John asked.

"Yes. Except for my servant, who came with me. For safety." John looked back at Mary Magdalene, unsure of what to do. "Will you let us in? We come in peace," said the distraught female voice from outside.

Mary Magdalene took a step toward John and nodded. John unbolted the door and cracked it a few inches. He could see a woman who looked to be in her mid-twenties standing outside. Behind her stood a tall older man, holding a torch above them both. The woman clutched an undersized leather pouch in her hands.

"Hello," said the woman. "As I mentioned, I have something quite special for the Mother of Jesus—it's more like a small miracle." Her eyes flickered from John's eyes to over his shoulder. "Is she here?"

Mary Magdalene hurried to the door and opened it wide. "Of course, you can come in. Please excuse our poor manners. Come in, quickly. Roman soldiers are everywhere."

John shut the door while the others murmured and encircled Veronica.

"My name is Mary of Magdalene, and these are my friends. We're all friends of Jesus and His Mother. Show us what you have."

"But I want to place it directly into the hands of the Mother of Jesus. Is she here?"

"She asked to be left alone," John said. "She just buried her Son, and she has not slept in two days. Unless you've brought something she would want to see right now, this second, I won't let you disturb her."

Veronica took a deep breath and then shared how she and her family had found themselves unexpectedly near Jesus as He staggered up the steps of Jerusalem carrying His cross. Seeing His face and eyes dripping with sweat and blood, she handed Him a linen face cloth she had planned to use herself because of the day's heat. Jesus had taken the cloth, quickly wiped his face, and given it back with a slight nod. Sensing she might be in danger if the guards noticed what had happened, she and her family slipped away and returned home.

"I hid the cloth from sight," she said, pointing at her leather pouch, "lest anyone question us. When we reached home, I kept this pouch for safe-keeping, but couldn't stop crying, thinking of the horrible things done to our Redeemer."

Mary Magdalene drew closer. "You're a believer."

Veronica nodded. "Later, when the tremors and lightening calmed, I opened the pouch and took out the cloth. The face of our Redeemer was staring back at me, and I felt this great calm come over me. I'm hoping it will do the same for His Mother."

"Thank you," John said quietly. "You may be the answer to her prayers." He walked to Mother Mary's bedroom, wiping his face on a sleeve, and knocked.

"Mother, it's me," he said loud enough so she could hear through the closed door. "A woman named Veronica is here with a gift for you. She says it's from Jesus, and she will only deliver it into your hands. She hopes it will bring you some peace and comfort."

Silence filled the room for a moment.

"Okay. Okay," Mother said barely above a whisper.

John rushed to her side to make sure she didn't try to walk. He wrapped one arm around her shoulder. "You don't need to stand up, Mother. Veronica will bring it."

Led by Mary Magdalene, the young woman entered Mother's bedroom and, without a word, knelt at her feet. She reached into her pouch and pulled out the white linen cloth and unfolded it for all to see. The face of Jesus covered nearly the entire fabric; He had a warm, reassuring smile on His face, absent any blood, face wounds, or crown of thorns.

Plucking the cloth from Veronica's hands, Mother Mary moaned with joy, clutching it to her bosom. She rolled back onto her side on the bed, sobbing. "Oh, my Son, my Son, my dear, dear Son... I will see You soon. You *are* coming back.

The room was silent around her.

She sniffled, looking around at everyone. "Years ago, when He was a boy, Joseph and I thought we had lost Him. We searched and searched and searched. We thought He was gone. But He was sitting with the Temple Elders. Talking to them of kindness. Of love. Now, I know He will come back to me. I don't have to search. I know I'm going to see Him again."

Mother Mary turned to everyone in her room. "Please let me be alone. . . I need to offer God many prayers of great thanks." Before everyone had completely filed out, she called out, "Thank you, Veronica, for bringing this. Thank you!" The woman paused in the doorway and smiled at Mary, shutting the door behind her as she left.

Mary clutched the cloth to her chest and closed her eyes. She could not cry anymore—she had no tears left. But if she had, these would be tears of joy. She would see her Son again.

Chapter Five

"Three times a year—on the Feast of Unleavened Bread, on the Feast of Weeks, and on the Feast of Booths—all your males shall appear before the Lord your God in the place that he will choose. They shall not appear before the Lord empty-handed." (Deuteronomy 16:16)

Mary and Joseph could only afford the 91-mile pilgrimage from Nazareth to Jerusalem once a year. After leaving Egypt and establishing themselves in their new home and community, they finally saved enough to take seven-year-old Jesus to Jerusalem for the Feast of Unleavened Bread for the first time. They joined a caravan of relatives and friends walking to Jerusalem for the Passover celebration. The journey would typically take about five days each way. Once in the city, they stayed with Joseph's relatives and their neighbors. He had been making this trip by himself for many years before he fell in love with Mary.

By the time Jesus had reached His twelfth year, Mary and Joseph knew that making the trip to Jerusalem for Passover with friends and neighbors was something Jesus looked forward to. He had developed an almost insatiable appetite for knowledge—about His people and faith, geography, the money system, what people worried about, what people thought about the Romans, what people thought about their Jewish leaders. His areas of interest knew no bounds.

Mary had also observed that Jesus knew the way to Jerusalem backwards and forwards and could easily guide their caravan if the need ever arose. The trip began along a small path out of Nazareth in a southeasterly direction that gently circled below the Sea of Galilee. Eventually, the road widened as it went downhill alongside the narrow Jordan. As the river widened, taking on various brooks and creeks, so did the road to Jerusalem widen where more people joined the Nazarenes.

Mary mused at how Jesus loved to run ahead and then run back past the women and children to the rear of the procession where His father and the rest of the men walked and talked among themselves. He'd listen awhile to their conversations and then run off again—sometimes even back to places where their group had already passed. Eventually the procession arrived at the Dead Sea, turned west near Jericho, and began the long climb up into the high country of Judea. Because of the steepness of the road, Jesus could easily run far ahead and wait for the Nazarene caravan. He had often told His parents how this gave Him plenty of time to think by Himself and observe the animals, birds, and reptiles of the area—He never ceased to be impressed at the complexity of the lives of all creatures.

Mary felt such strong delight for her quickly maturing son, but whenever she saw that sparkling joy and wonder in His eyes, she forced herself to conceal her feelings. She and Joseph had made a pact that they would never brag or call attention to their incredible Son's gifts—that was not their job. But still. Her heart almost burst with love every time He used His gifts. He always used them to help or to heal, covertly bringing animals and birds back to life when He thought no one was looking.

On the evening of the fifth day, Jerusalem finally came into view. Mary, Joseph, and Jesus had once again spent the previous night on makeshift cots inside a large tent next to a busy roadside inn just like they had the three previous nights. None of them had gotten much sleep since they left Nazareth, but Jesus and the rest of the children in the caravan never ran out of energy. So they clapped and jumped with glee at the sight of the gleaming Holy City.

A long twisting road had yet to be traversed before the Nazarenes would arrive inside those majestic high walls, but in no way did that reality diminish the splendor of the view. Endless rows of camps surrounded the walls with multi-colored tents of all shapes and sizes with cooking fires that blazed through the morning haze. With the crush of so many coming to the city, Joseph insisted that Jesus walk close to him, where he could see Him at all times.

Mary didn't want her family getting separated and decided to walk with them as well. She'd been making the journey to Jerusalem for much of her married life, and each time she saw the Temple, she couldn't help but gasp at its magnificence—its monumental size and grandeur stretched left and right as far as the eye could see and towered up into the heavens, white and gold finishes shimmering in the sunlight.

Jesus was twelve now and could join the men in the Hall of the Israelites inside the Temple, but couldn't make His Bar Mitzvah until He was thirteen. On that day, He would be recognized as ready to assume the responsibilities of manhood and to take part in public worship. But for today, Mary couldn't wait to get to the home of Joseph's relatives. It had been a long and tedious journey with so many from Nazareth—the numbers increased dramatically each year, as did the constant noises, day and night.

Mary never fared well without a few hours of deep sleep on these journeys. And she had begun to worry lately. She wasn't sure what she was worried about, but the nagging worry would not be silenced, even in those rare moments when all the other noises of traveling ceased.

For the people of Nazareth, the Passover celebration filled their minds and hearts with inspiration and rejuvenation. Twelve-year-old Jesus found quiet moments where he could hide out of sight in the Hall of the Israelites and listen to the teachers and men from His village discussing their faith. His stepfather asked good questions, but the more Jesus heard, the more He wanted to know. Next year He would be thirteen and could read in the Temple, but for now He still had too many unanswered questions.

After their eighth day in the city, the Nazarenes began their return journey. The women and children left the city first because of their slow pace, and the men and older boys would generally catch up around dinner time, well before it was time to bed down for the night. So when Joseph and the other males finally caught up with the women near Jericho, only then did Mary and Joseph realize that Jesus had not traveled with the men.

So where was He?

They spent the rest of that night asking the families in their caravan if they had seen the boy after leaving Jerusalem, but no one had. There seemed only two reasonable conclusions: the boy had decided to stay behind or someone had kidnapped Him, either in Jerusalem or along the road out of Jerusalem. The road between Jerusalem and Jericho had a reputation for bandits and robbers, desperate people who would attack, take what they could, and then disappear into the desert.

Mary and Joseph wasted no time. They packed a pouch of food and a skin of water, lit a torch, and began the journey back to Jerusalem in the dark. They fully understood the dangers of traveling at night, but they had to reach Joseph's family as quickly as possible. They would help organize a search throughout the city once Mary and Joseph got there, but until they arrived back in Jerusalem, their Son could be anywhere.

The couple walked in silence using their walking sticks for almost an hour before Joseph finally spoke.

"Mary," he said quietly, "Please accept my sincerest apology. I'm so sorry. I didn't check to make sure He was in the caravan. I was so wrapped up talking about a year from now and His thirteenth birthday with the others. Jesus has always been so responsible and thoughtful. It just never dawned on me that He might stay behind. What could He have been thinking?"

"I should have been keeping an eye out for Him as well," Mary said matter-of-factly. "Besides, we don't *know* that He decided to leave us."

She stopped speaking and they walked in silence for awhile.

"Maybe someone took Him?" she said finally, voice cracking. "Maybe someone wants money for our Son. Maybe they've already sold Him. I'm sure there's a black market for that."

"Don't say that."

"Or what if someone's killed Him? With so many people coming to the city, who knows what evil some men may have in their hearts?"

Her voice kept rising and she waved both arms as she spoke.

"And now our Son is missing because His parents had too many other things on their minds coming back from Passover."

She wiped a sleeve across Her eyes.

Joseph placed an arm around her. "It's going to be alright, Mary. We'll find our Son, and He'll be fine. I'm sure it's just a misunderstanding—you'll see."

The next day's sun blazed toward an early sunset as the couple finally arrived in Jerusalem and rushed to Joseph's family home.

After gulping some fresh water, they contritely explained how it had come to pass that they lost track of their Son. Joseph's family, neighbors, and friends quickly organized a search party that lasted the rest of the afternoon.

When everyone had reassembled, it was dark. Mary and Joseph felt on the verge of despair until one of Joseph's brothers mentioned almost as a afterthought that he had observed Jesus eavesdropping in the Hall of the Israelites days ago while the teachers and learned men of Nazareth discussed Mosaic Law. Maybe someone at Temple might have noticed Him.

Joseph had barely suggested they look there before Mary had bolted from her seat and into the streets toward the Temple, Joseph's family in hot pursuit. Unconcerned for who she ran into, she shouted into the dark, "Jesus! Jesus, where are you, Son? Jesus!"

Once at the Temple, she raced past Solomon's Porch, the Court of the Gentiles, the Soreg, up the steps and through the Beautiful Gate, and finally into the Court of Women. As she dashed toward the Nicanor Gate, which could only legally be entered by adult Jewish males going to the Hall of Israelites, she heard a clamor of voices from inside the Hall.

Seemingly confused, Jesus walked out through the Gate toward his Mother, elders and teachers of the Temple close behind. "What's the matter, Mother?" He said, clearly distressed over her apparent state of panic. "Why are you shouting for me?"

Just then Joseph caught up with his wife, soaked in sweat and out of breath. "What do you mean, 'What's the *matter*?'" Joseph wheezed. "You've been missing for three days!"

"*Missing*?" the boy said, voice rising in disbelief.

"He's been here with us," one of the elders volunteered. "His understanding and knowledge of scripture and the Law far exceed his age. If I were His parent, I'd be most proud."

49

Mary took a deep breath, crossed her arms, and studied her astonished twelve-year-old. His hair was growing long and He now stood almost as tall as Joseph.

"You mean to tell us," she said, "that You had no idea that we might be upset? That we might be scared out of our wits? That we might be afraid for your safety?"

Jesus shrugged, His eyes genuine in their confusion. "No, I did not. I'm very sorry. Did you not know that I must be in my Father's house?"

Mary and Joseph exchanged a quick frown of confusion and ran to Jesus, wrapping their arms around their Son, who was growing up far too quickly.

"We're just so happy we've found You and that You're safe," Joseph whispered. "We love you so very much, dear Son!" Still short of breath, he then gave Mary a warm kiss on the cheek. "And thank you, dear wife, for your many kindnesses. I hope you know how much I appreciate and love you." And looking up at the heavens, he said, "Thank you, dear God, for keeping us all safe. You are indeed merciful."

Jesus pulled back and studied His parents—a peaceful smile on His face.

Mary noted the boy's look of relief at apparently having resolved His parents' distress. She memorized that moment into the deep recesses of her heart and soul. Something told her that she would one day need to recall it.

———◦※◦———

THE CENACLE
UPPER FLOOR BEDROOM OF MOTHER MARY
EVENING OF THE SABBATH
33 AD
THE FIRST DAY

Mary awoke with the expression of her twelve-year-old's face from 21 years earlier flickering through her thoughts. She opened her eyes just enough to see her grown Son's face smiling from the white cloth given her by Veronica.

She took a deep breath. "Thank You, dear Son," she whispered, "I now know You're not totally gone from my life, and that I will soon see You again. I love You more than I could ever find the right words to say. If only Joseph were here to help me figure out the mess Pilate and Caiaphas have made of Your beautiful message. It's going to take a lot of hard work, and lots of prayer, and I have no idea where to begin, but I know You'll help—somehow. . . "

As she closed her eyes and felt herself drifting back into the comforting arms of much-needed sleep, an old loneliness crept out of a corner of her heart. She'd been quietly wrestling with this grief ever since her Joseph had passed. Usually, she could push it from her thoughts, but as she sank toward deep unconsciousness, the ache of her husband's absence refused to rest.

Joseph had always been a man of infectious virtue, a good father, and a deeply loving friend—as well as a strong, protective, and reliable man of God. They'd been together almost 30 years, going back to when she had just turned fourteen. Five years ago, God had decided it was time to bring her wonderful husband into His loving presence.

He'd been sick for almost ten years before, but his stoic, thoughtful, and occasionally stubborn nature made him slow to show his pain. A few years before his passing, the whole family agreed that it was too dangerous for him to work in the woodshop, given his health problems. Reluctantly, he spent his days at home with Mary while Jesus kept up the family carpentry business.

Even ill, Joseph would ask Mary every day how he could help with the household chores or the preparation of meals. Mary delighted in finding meaningful tasks for him, and it was during these final years that the couple again became best friends. In the years since their wedding, they'd both been so consumed with holding up their family duties and responsibilities that they barely had energy enough to observe the amenities toward each other.

Despite Joseph's failing health, Mary had been thrilled by their daily camaraderie and rekindled friendship. He had always been good company—something she'd missed from her childhood. Her parents had left her at the Temple at age three, and thereafter her life had focused all its energy toward service to God. Until her fourteenth year, she knew virtually no human warmth, and certainly no kind touch—not even a hug—only service and responsibilities. Each night, she would sleep on the earthen floor and arise during the night to pray along with the other girls from Jerusalem who had voluntarily made similar commitments. She loved God with all her being, but her loneliness throughout childhood had sapped the feeling of rapture from her service for the Lord. She had learned to push such thoughts from her mind.

In Mary's fourteenth year, Joseph came calling at the Temple, looking for a wife who shared his commitment to a life of service to the Lord. As they slowly got to know each other, she found herself falling in love with this wonderful older man. Tall, strong, and ruggedly good-looking, he always exuded a peaceful and understated confidence in his ability to handle any unexpected challenges life sent his way.

If only Joseph could be here now, to hold her and comfort her.

Mary tossed and turned in her bed and felt herself aching in her heart for her Joseph. He would know what to do. He would know whom to trust.

The insidiously quick trial and murder of her Son by Caiaphas and his associates had left her feeling exposed and vulnerable. Jesus had warned her, and His followers, that He would soon die. But none of them dreamed it could happen with such speed and blatant disregard of the Law. The grisly terror of it all caused the Apostles and disciples to scatter to the wind, into hiding from Roman soldiers the Chief Priest and his cabal had commissioned to capture, kill, and make an example of Jesus before all Jerusalem.

If only Joseph were here now, she told herself, he would maintain his composure while helping her and the Apostles make sense of this nightmarish Passover. Mary felt tears running down her cheeks. She knew she wasn't her usual reserved self. Had she slept? She felt as though she had been run over by a runaway horse and chariot. But this was no time for self-pity. She was going to have to figure out what she should do right now to make sure what her Jesus had started remained alive and growing.

But she couldn't do it by herself.

"Dear Father in Heaven," she whispered, "please help me know what to do."

Elsewhere on the same floor, Mary Clopas advised Magdalena to get some sleep. But Mary Magdalene couldn't stop thinking about all the difficult planning that needed to be considered and put into action. She kept whispering at the others in the room and pacing the floor where Jesus had eaten His final meal only last night. Like all adult Jews, Magdalene understood how the Sabbath needed to be a day of rest. But she also believed that merely collecting materials and spices for the completion of a proper burial for an executed man could not be considered labor and therefore would be within the Law. The burial laws of their faith allowed for a temporary burial when death occurred just prior to the arrival of the Sabbath. The temporary burial would need to be made permanent as soon as possible—Sunday at dawn, as soon as the Sabbath night ended.

Magdalena could hear whispers from those around her, their eyes following her. No doubt they wondered if she had lost her wits watching the brutal torture and murder of her dear friend and teacher. It had long been recognized among Jesus' disciples that the Magdalene had become one of Jesus' favorites.

"Why do you pace and mumble so?" said Mary of Zebedee.

"Because there's much to do."

"What are you talking about?" said Martha.

"We must finish burying Jesus."

"With what?" Joanna said.

"We need many pounds of aloe and myrrh. There was not enough oil in the tomb, so He was badly washed."

"I agree," said Mary of Clopas, "but not now. It's the Sabbath."

"I will get them."

"I will go with you for protection," John said.

"You're needed here for Mother Mary. I will go by myself. I know about such things."

"Have you taken leave of your senses?" blurted Mary of Clopas.

"Roman soldiers are everywhere," added Mary of Bethany. "They're on the prowl for any friends of Jesus or Lazarus!"

"I *must* go with you," John said. "Remember what the soldiers at the tomb said?"

"I forbid it!" said his mother, Mary of Zebedee.

"I'm leaving" said Mary Magdalene, reaching for her mantle.

"You're crazy to go out alone," said Martha. "You're just inviting disaster. They might arrest and torture you to find Lazarus. They hate him and the rest of us nearly as much as Jesus."

Magdalena shook her head in dismay.

"What's happened to your courage of these past three years? Tonight we saw the Roman soldiers in action. These are not evil men, merely men doing their jobs so they can get home to their families. They were just going through the motions of carrying out orders from Pilate and the Sanhedrin. They could have stopped and questioned us; they wouldn't even need a legal reason. But pestering grieving Jews isn't high on their list of priorities. Their greatest concern—what the Romans and the Chief Priests both fear most—is civil unrest. And they're not going to chance that during the Holy Days."

Mary Magdalene looked around the room expecting someone to disagree. When no one did, she put on her mantle, threw a burlap sack over her shoulder, and disappeared alone into the darkness.

CHAPTER SIX

THE PILATE RESIDENCE
JERUSALEM
THE SABBATH
LATE EVENING (11-12 PM)
33 AD
THE FIRST DAY

"While Pilate was still seated on the bench, his wife sent him a message, 'Have nothing to do with that righteous man. I suffered much in a dream today because of him.'" (Matthew 27:19)

Pontius Pilate paced the living room of his Jerusalem home—he didn't like how things had turned out that day.

The tall and beautiful Procula entered and sat in silence, watching her husband's striding. She took a deep breath, expecting he would soon begin to berate her, as was his habit whenever she did something of which he did not approve. The young woman came from patrician blood as the granddaughter of the Emperor Augustus. Procula's trim figure and reputation as an accomplished seer had fascinated Pilate from the moment they met. He had been 27 when she was seventeen; and his sleek grace had reminded young Procula of a leopard. Within a year, they married and moved to Judea. Both saw Pilate's new appointment as an opportunity for rapid promotion.

The official and most luxurious residence of the procurator stood in the palace of Herod west of Jerusalem in the nearby city of Cæsarea, where a military force of about 3,000 soldiers remained at the ready around the clock. Pilate had ordered these troops to Jerusalem for Passover because he knew that the city would soon swell with thousands of Jewish families making their annual pilgrimage as prescribed by Mosaic Law. This predictable and present danger to his successful governance motivated Pilate and Procula to also come to Jerusalem in the spring.

In the seven years since Pilate's arrival, he had ruled all Judea and Jerusalem with an iron fist, thus ensuring that his yearly reports to Rome overflowed with glowing accounts of his many successes in controlling the Jewish lower class. Luckily, there was considerable cooperation from the local Jewish hierarchy—the Holy Men of the Temple did all they could to stay in Pilate's good graces. The particular tactics Pilate used to rule over this jurisdiction were of no interest to his superiors—only that he met their taxation quotas and kept "the peace" within the Jewish community, something his predecessors had often failed to achieve.

As he paced deep in thought, Pilate came to the disturbing realization that his future career might be in serious jeopardy as a result of the events of yesterday. There seemed little he could do to change the disastrous path he had stumbled into. He had barely noticed when Procula had joined him, but now he saw a ray of light. Abruptly, he stopped striding and turned to face her. "Tell me of your dream about the Nazarene."

"What about it?"

"Your note said the dream has caused you great distress? What distress?"

"I've always told you about my dreams, but you don't listen. I've been having the same dream for years, but last night—for the first time—I could see that it was the Nazarene Jesus who had been haunting my dreams with his blood."

"What happened?"

"It was horrible. A mute and blood-covered almost-naked man staggered and fell on both of us while we reclined at dinner. In previous dreams, I could never see his face—just the caked blood in his long hair; his back oozed blood from scores of lashings. He collapsed on us and drenched us in blood, but again I could never see his face. Then I would wake up, and you'd be sound asleep. I've always told you about my dreams—this one was especially disturbing."

"So what was different about last night?"

"I saw his face as he was falling on us, but his eyes remained closed. He kept saying, 'Forgive them, for they know not what they do' over and over. That's when I knew who it was. My new friend, Mary Magdalene, introduced me to Jesus months ago."

"You never told me about that."

"Why should I? You hate the Jews."

Pilate stared back at her and took a deep breath. "I don't hate them. I just want them to behave and stop causing me trouble in Rome. Remember, Sejanus was a friend. Sejanus liked me and made sure my reputation in Rome remained spotless. But Tiberius had him murdered. And now, Tiberius has decided to rule by himself and sent orders that the Jews should be handled with kindness. But their elders wanted Jesus dead! If I hadn't kept Caiaphas and his friends happy, they would have sent emissaries to Rome complaining of my lack of understanding for the needs of their community."

Procula rolled her eyes. "You keep talking as if Jesus created political problems. He didn't. His words posed no threat to Rome or you. His teachings emphasized love and compassion and the hypocrisy of current Jewish leadership. You were sent here with the judicial power to enforce political solutions—where appropriate—to the problems of Judea."

"But he said he was 'King of the Jews.'"

"So what? Tiberius doesn't care who the Jews say their king is as long as they don't try to challenge the authority of Rome. Jesus never did that."

Pilate sat down across from his young wife and smiled at her stunning beauty. "So you're saying Jesus was an innocent man?"

"I'm saying Jesus posed no threat to Roman rule and should have been set free."

"What about Caiaphas and his followers in the Sanhedrin? They wanted him dead, and if I didn't order him crucified, they expressed fear of rioting in the streets."

"You have 3,000 troops here at your disposal. You could easily have arrested, convicted, and crucified Caiaphas and his crowd for inciting to riot—using their own words to convict. You had the legal power and the manpower to enforce your will, but you walked right into their trap. That's what I was trying to help you avoid. Now you're going to have to defend yourself with Tiberius about having crucified an innocent Jew."

Procula stood and began pacing. "From Rome's point of view, what you did yesterday was to allow yourself to be maneuvered by Caiaphas into becoming an enforcement tool for him and his power-hungry accomplices. They will come to you again, soon, claiming they don't have the authority to enforce their own laws because each new case will be about 'preserving the peace.' They'll keep hounding at you until you put a stop to it."

Pilate nodded slowly. "You're right. They've already talked me into using those Roman troops to search for friends of Jesus all over the city, but those people have gone into hiding. We'll never find them. What they really want is for me to capture and crucify that man Lazarus—Jesus is supposed to have brought him back to life. But we both know that's not possible, but if word gets out that it is, the result could mean real trouble for the Chief Priest."

Procula sat down beside her husband and took both his hands in hers and looked him in the eye. "My dear husband, I love you. My note today was an attempt to warn you about Caiaphas and his trap. Caiaphas and the Jewish leaders will try to *use you* again. It's just a matter of when."

Pilate looked down and slowly shook his head. "I have no doubt you're right. Caiaphas is a ruthless snake. I should have heeded your warning. I have no idea what to do next."

Procula placed an arm around his shoulders and gave him a gentle kiss on the cheek. "Don't worry, husband. You and I, and Isis will think of something."

Pilate squinted and fell into deep thought. He nodded his head as though he had just had an important insight. "Tell me more about this Mary Magdalene person," he said, his disposition becoming sunny. "Do you trust her?" The beginnings of a self-satisfied grin crept into one side of his mouth. "And tell me what you know about Jewish burial law."

━━●━◦✳◦━●━━

UPPER ROOM
EARLY MORNING OF THE SABBATH
EIGHTH HOUR OF THE NIGHT (ABOUT 2 AM)
THE FIRST DAY

The Apostle John tried to stop worrying about what might happen to Mary Magdalene alone on the streets of Jerusalem. He would feel better about it if she had permitted him to come with her. But he had to stay in the Upper Room to comfort and reassure Mother Mary once she finally awoke. He blinked away the heaviness growing over his head. He would need to sleep soon himself. But he would stay awake until Mary Magdalene returned.

Her bravery as she had left did nothing to relieve the knot in John's stomach. He knew that great danger lurked on the streets for any follower of Jesus. Pilate had ordered his soldiers to maintain a strong visible presence around the city and be on the lookout for anyone likely to have been associated with Jesus. Caiaphas and the leaders of the Sanhedrin would keep trying to convince the governor that friends of the Nazarene had plans to incite a riot.

But none in this room would have given the Romans any trouble. Even if they'd wanted to, all the faces in the room looked weary. Defeated. The women who remained on this floor after Magdala left moved into their own quiet corners and private thoughts, praying silently while crying as noiselessly as they could. It was impossible to fathom all that had happened to their leader that day—so quickly, so mercilessly, so finally. After all the many miracles they had witnessed in His presence during the past months and years, John thought it was all leading toward something. Now, in less than a day, Jesus had been murdered and buried.

"Why did He let this happen?" John heard Mary Clopas whispering on her knees. As sister to Mother Mary, John knew that she had witnessed many unexplainable things Jesus had said and done since He was a boy. But Jesus allowing himself to be murdered made no sense at all—especially to the new son of Mother Mary.

Jesus had warned all of them, but none took His words literally—He spoke so often in parables, it was hard to tell what He meant sometimes. He had asked John to care for and protect Mother Mary; but John had no idea what that meant. He had never had to be responsible for anyone else before. All he really knew was the fishing he learned from his father and brother and their partners and friends, Andrew and Peter: to always keep his word and be responsible for his own actions. Now he'd been suddenly thrust into an adult-sized job—something for which he had no training. Why was this his burden when he was the only one who hadn't run away? Where had all the other Apostles gone?

———◆◦※◦◆———

The Streets of Jerusalem
Ninth Hour of the Night (3 AM)
The First Day

Mary Magdalene had learned to blend into the nighttime shadows of Jerusalem long before she met Jesus. As an itinerate house servant (and thief when necessary), she knew the city's upper-class families like the palms of her hands. She had committed to memory the addresses and mindsets of many of the elite—especially as it concerned when they would remain or go into hiding during high Jewish holidays. Many such families routinely closed their luxurious estates to avoid the predictable chaos the religious pilgrims brought with them, especially during Passover.

To the best of Magdalene's knowledge, such families had no reason to substantially alter their traditional family behavior. She reasoned that connecting with some of her old servant friends who had been left behind in their employers' upper-class homes should be fairly easy. But it was also true that she hadn't been in close contact with most of her servant friends for several years. She worried that she might be unable to collect the necessary fresh linens, spices, herbs, aloe, and myrrh at one address. She shrugged in the darkness and kept reminding herself that with God's help all things were possible.

A steady stream of whispered prayers passed her lips while she tried to convince herself that she would remain unnoticed by any Roman soldiers tonight. Reassuring herself that the Jewish leaders and Pilate feared crowds more than individuals, Magdalene employed all her old street skills to slip in and out of the city's early morning shadows, taking particular care to give the appearance to untrained eyes of being homeless, drunk, or lost.

The barking of trained hunting dogs straining at their leashes shattered the quiet darkness, followed by the clatter of horses advancing toward Magdalene's hiding place behind a building. Once the shadowy figures made their way onto the moonlit street, she could see at least six soldiers on horseback, accompanied by five rottweilers and their handlers.

"Who goes there?" demanded a loud male voice above the snarling dog sounds.

Magdalene wasn't sure what to do, so she said nothing and froze in place.

"We know where you're hiding, but have no desire to turn these dogs loose on you. Show and identify yourself if you want to be treated fairly," said the same insistent voice, strangely familiar.

Magdalene raised her hands and walked out of the shadows and into the middle of the street. My name is Mary of Magdala and I'm on my way to visit friends."

"Really?" said the same voice as its owner advanced toward her on his large black horse. "Going to visit friends at this hour?"

Magdalene now recognized the man. Her blood pounded in her ears.

CHAPTER SEVEN

For Joseph of Arimathea, the events of the past 24 hours belonged in a nightmare—one he prayed he could dismiss from his thoughts. In all his travels around the world—especially in Rome with the many horrors he'd observed there—he could not remember ever witnessing the magnitude of hatred one man held for another as Caiaphas had for Jesus.

The chief priest reminded Joseph of a mad dog, foaming at the mouth with an overwhelming rage for the complete dismemberment and destruction of an innocent who had no part in the dog's illness. No, the malice Caiaphas had for Jesus could not be based on anything He had ever said or done. Jesus was about love, so it had to go deeper than that. Perhaps it had its genesis in a fear of an imagined threat to the office of Chief Priest, and the resultant loss of income from the covert arrangement Caiaphas had with the Romans. Joseph wasn't supposed to know about that arrangement, but most of the Sanhedrin knew—they just never spoke of it.

That's why Joseph knew he had to move far away from Jerusalem. The dishonesty of those who were supposed to be

64

leading the Jewish people in their faith knew no bounds.

But Joseph had to push these distracting thoughts from his mind, focus on the task at hand. Preparing for the proper burial of Jesus on Sunday. He owed Jesus and His family that much. But he was unsure of his own stamina.

Disposition of the seamless tunic Mary had made for Jesus, which one of Joseph's servants had found on Golgotha, would have to wait until after the final burial of Jesus on Sunday.

The moon provided scant light for him to find his way along the dark streets of Jerusalem and he often glanced to each side for reassurance that his most fierce and trustworthy servants walked just behind him. His eldest son, family, and friends walked well behind and on the opposite side of the street. Shortly after their surprise encounter with a regretful and well-disguised centurion, Joseph and his group rearranged their garments so as to look like Passover visitors. The commander had warned that Caiaphas had hired Pagan soldiers to attack and seize anyone with even the slightest connection to Jesus.

Joseph barely had enough strength left to complete his journey home, but the threat of an attack by soldiers kept him upright. He tried to maintain appearances with a measured steady pace now that he was mere blocks from his home. He dared not show any overt sign of concern; those in his entourage already feared for his safety and had insisted on staying with him once he left Jesus' tomb.

There was so much to think about that neither Joseph nor his family and friends noticed the silent movements of covert men on foot, noiselessly leading their horses, and all concealed by the shadows afforded by the dark street. With a clatter of hooves and jangling steel, a group of armed men charged at Joseph, knocked his guards senseless, then seized and the gagged older gentleman.

The last thing Joseph saw before being carried off was his

friends and family scattering into the night like panicked animals of the forest.

JERUSALEM
CENACLE HOUSE (UPPER ROOM)
EARLY DAWN OF THE SABBATH (LATE FOURTH WATCH)
33 AD
THE FIRST DAY

Following the noisy incident on the city streets on Passover concerning the Nazarene, the serenity of the Sabbath now provided perfect cover for a new strategy by the Sanhedrin—a full-on covert search for any and all followers of Jesus. Now that the followers of Jesus had also scattered and gone into hiding, the Temple leaders felt certain their shared power and cash arrangements with the Romans would remain intact.

Pilate had held up his end of the bargain with the Jewish elders by ordering his soldiers to provide a "for show only" use of force along its streets and back alleys. Whatever the Nazarene had inspired in His followers, these common Judeans would have no interest now in confronting Roman soldiers. Word had spread about the vicious brutality inflicted on the Nazarene and His two crucifixion companions.

The city had quieted in anticipation of a new day that would also be the Sabbath. When the cock finally crowed, the long night ended, and the daylight portion of the Sabbath began.

Jesus' followers inside the Cenacle took little notice of the first rays of the day. Most of the city's inhabitants slept through the dawn, but not John. He still had not slept—he had much too much on his mind. Luckily, the whole building was quiet and his frantic thoughts had begun to calm and focus on the problems at hand.

What should I be doing to help Mother Mary? There must be something. And what about Mary Magdalene? She's most likely been arrested by the Romans—who knows what those savage hyenas may have done to her? Of all people, she should have known the danger. Why would she go out like that? Before sunrise?

A loud knocking interrupted his thoughts. John took a deep breath and wiped his face, hoping that whoever it was would go away. But another knocking came, louder. The women in the room began to shake their heads in agonized despair; John knew their fears. They fully expected more bad news or maybe it was the Romans coming to make arrests.

John rose from his knees, blew his nose, and walked slowly toward the bolted door.

"Who is it?" the teenager asked in a loud whisper, trying not to awaken Mother Mary. He wondered if he should have said anything until the visitor announced their name.

"It's me, Mary of Magdalene," a familiar voice said from outside the door. "Open up, John. I've got an incredible and wonderful surprise for everyone."

The women in the room looked at each other, eyes wide, and ran for the front door. "Mary, Mary," they whispered. John unbolted the door and swung it open.

Everyone fell silent. Two large men who looked like someone's powerful man-servants stood behind Magdalene, each carrying several bulging bags over their shoulders.

"Who are these men?" John asked.

Magdalene shrugged. "My friends allowed me to borrow them so they could carry all the spices we're going to need to complete the burial tomorrow."

"Oh," he muttered, unable to think of a clever reply. He motioned for Mary and her borrowed servants to enter. "So you've got everything you set out to find?"

"I have." Magdala pointed where she wanted the men to set their bags on the floor. "Thank you, gentlemen. You have our sincerest gratitude."

The men who brought the spices left quickly and John closed the door and bolted it behind them.

"You were gone so long, we had begun to fear the worst," John said.

Mary Magdalene glanced around the room at her fellow disciples—male and female. She took a deep breath, then spoke slowly and deliberately. "I know how you feel. I feared the worst tonight many times myself. Like you, my heart is broken. Like you, I am unsure of who we can trust. We all love Jesus and that will never stop. What has happened to Him is... well, it's beyond words. Like the loving gift each of you is to me, Jesus was a gift, from God, for all of us and all the people of this world. But now He's been cruelly ripped away."

She paused to look into the eyes of everyone.

"Nonetheless, we still have to carry on His work as best we can. And that journey begins by making sure He has a proper burial. And that means we still have a lot of work to do. That does not mean denying our grief. For some, that will mean continuing to weep. But our tears are not going to change the work that still needs doing. We can cry and work too."

Pointing to the bags on the floor, she said. "We have to grind all these ugly balls of myrrh into powder by dawn tomorrow. That's the only way we can give Jesus the proper burial He deserves."

John knelt beside the animal-skin bags and began isolating those swelled with lumps of myrrh or bulging with mortar and pestle implements.

"Where did you get all this?" he asked.

The Magdala shrugged and smirked impishly at the boy. "Friends."

"Friends?" he repeated, scowling. "That's it?"

"There's no need for anyone to know any more than that. Everyone here has the right to protect benefactors of the followers of Jesus who wish to remain anonymous." Seeing he was still unconvinced, she continued, "No one followed us, if that's what you're worried about."

A booming knock on the front door interrupted them.

All the women except Magdalene looked to the door in wide-eyed panic. This was it. The Romans had found them. John stared at the woman from Magdala, seething with contempt. She glared back. "Is there something you want to say?"

The loud knocking continued.

John didn't take his eyes off Magdalene, clenching his jaw muscles. "Looks like you're not nearly as clever as you think," he hissed.

"Are you going to answer the door," she asked, "or are you going to wait until someone breaks it down?" He rushed to the door, Magdalene close behind.

"Who is it?" John said loudly through the door, trying to make his voice sound deeper and more authoritative.

A naturally deep male voice nervously cleared his throat. "My name is Centurion Cassius Longinus, and I've been sent by Joseph of Arimathea."

"The same Centurion Longinus in charge of crucifixions? What would make you think you would be welcome here?"

"I understand your anger." He paused. "Joseph said I should bring them anyway."

John shook his head and turned to face Magdalene in silence.

"Are you alone?" John asked.

"Yes."

"For what purpose do you come to this house?" John demanded, still glaring at Mary.

"I have brought some of the personal effects of Jesus. His mother specifically requested them, according to Joseph. He has at least one more that he's going to bring later."

He turned to Magdalene. "You know anything about this?"

She nodded. "It's okay, John. Open the door. Mother Mary did ask Joseph to go looking for Jesus' personal effects during the walk back here from the sepulcher."

John frowned, but opened the door.

Longinus was alone. He wore no military attire but was dressed in a short gray tunic under a dark mantle, a leather pouch in his arms. He studied John and Mary. "I don't mean to disturb."

"You've got a lot of nerve coming here after what you've done!" John blurted.

"Excuse our poor manners," Magdalene said, pulling the door completely open for the tall muscular man to enter. "We've not slept much since learning that Roman soldiers are under orders to kill us. So you can understand if we're a bit on edge about Romans who knock on our door—and especially when it's you."

"This was the man who gave orders to the soldiers on Golgotha to torture and kill our Jesus!" John shouted out to the room.

Longinus just stood there, looking straight ahead then bowed his head in shame. "I don't blame you for hating me. I fear this is blood on my hands I will never be able to wash away. I was under strict orders from Pontius Pilate. I'm not excusing what I did, but you have no idea what it's like serving under him, every day. He'd kill my family if I didn't follow his orders."

He paused and for a whole minute no one spoke.

Finally Longinus lowered his eyes to the leather pouch in his arms. "As requested by Joseph, I've brought what I could find of the personal effects Jesus wore yesterday." He swallowed a lump in his throat. "The soldiers fought over them but later cast them aside. I've also brought a part of the lance I was ordered to use to make sure Jesus had died."

A door opened and everyone's heads turned. A squinting and disheveled Mother Mary shuffled into the central room, her long salt-and-pepper hair matted against one side of her head. Her sleeping garment had wrinkled and sweat covered her face and seeped through onto her chest and under her arms.

"What was that loud knocking?" she said, rubbing both eyes.

John and the women rushed to give assistance to the older woman, but Magdalene got there first and quickly explained that Joseph had sent Longinus to their door with the articles Mother Mary had requested, and that it was the centurion who had made the loud knocking. She also detailed how Longinus had been forced into service by Pilate.

"You!" exclaimed Mother Mary, glaring at Longinus. She studied him for a moment, shook her head slowly, and whispered, "Our friend Joseph must think highly of you to send you here on such a mission. How is it that you know Joseph?"

"I was searching the streets for where you all might be hiding when I spotted him walking with friends and some servants he had used on Golgotha. I told him that I wanted to find you and beg your forgiveness for what I had done. He told me I would not be welcome if I did not help in your search for your son's belongings," he said, looking down at his leather pouch. "Joseph then explained how he was going to try and locate as many of the Apostles as he could and tell them that the Mother of Jesus forgave them. Joseph also told me that he thought all the followers of Jesus needed to come together and be in this place, with the Mother of Jesus. He then wished me well, and we went our separate ways."

No one spoke.

Longinus looked down at the floor, "I'm so very sorry to have awakened you, Mother of Jesus," he said almost inaudibly. "I didn't think you would be asleep. Please forgive me—for that and all of my horrible deeds." Tears began to run down his face. "I'm so very, very sorry."

Mother Mary walked over to the tall, muscular young man and wrapped her arms around his thick waist. "Of course you're forgiven," she said and began to weep. Trying to regain control, she choked between her tears. "We all need to be forgiven—we who stood by and did nothing; the Apostles and followers who dared not help Him; and even Judas, who thought he knew best." She pulled a cloth from her sleeve, wiped her face, and blew her nose. "We all need to be forgiven." She pushed the hair back off of her face. "Now, Centurion Longinus, let us have a look at what you've brought."

———— ✦✦✦ ————

JERUSALEM
THE PERSONAL RESIDENCE OF PONTIUS PILATE
EARLY DAWN OF THE SABBATH (LATE FOURTH WATCH)
33 AD
THE FIRST DAY

Caiaphas and his small delegation from the Sanhedrin were all pacing or sitting nervously, awaiting the arrival of Pilate. They had come to the governor's home at this early hour in response to an emergency summons from Pilate.

Annas, father-in-law to Caiaphas, had placed himself in the seat of honor, representing the supreme judicial and ecclesiastical council. At the moment he was facing straight ahead, eyes closed, and shaking his head.

Irritated by his father-in-law, Caiaphas could no longer keep quiet. "Annas," he blurted, "why are you shaking your head?"

"Because, we should never have come here," Annas whispered.

"This whole so-called secret, emergency meeting is bad business. I feel it in my bones."

As if on cue, Pilate and his wife entered the room, accompanied by several of the Procurator's top staff and Chuza, acting Commander of the Palace Guard.

"Good morning, gentlemen of Judea," Pilate began while taking a moment to quickly study his guests. "You may be wondering why I thought this meeting so important that I picked such an early hour." He turned to Annas. "You think it was a mistake to come here, Annas? You feel it in your bones?"

The older man stood and bowed politely toward Pilate. "I beg your pardon, sire, I was just thinking out loud."

Pilate nodded. "You may be right." He paused and took a deep breath. "Tell me something, Annas: Who am I?"

Annas scowled and looked at the others, hoping for a clue as to what Pilate meant. "I'm sorry, governor, I don't understand your question." He paused, desperately trying to choose words that would not offend. "The obvious answer is that you're the governor of all Judea."

Pilate nodded. "You're exactly right, Annas. And who are you?"

"Why are you asking me these questions, the answers to which you already know?"

Pilate put his arms behind his back and began pacing. "Answer my question, Annas."

"Well," Annas began, "I'm actually a nobody. I used to be High Priest of the Temple but was removed from office by procurator Valerius Gratus some eighteen years ago. Since then I've been in semi-retirement—but remain available for consultation."

"Why are you cross examining my father-in-law?" Caiaphas suddenly barked in anger. "Has he broken any Roman laws?"

"Keep quiet, Caiaphas," Pilate growled through clenched teeth. "You're next. You'd do well to pay close attention and listen.

Annas: do you have legal command over any soldiers—Roman or otherwise?"

"No, sir."

"Then perhaps you'd be so kind as to explain how it came to pass that you ordered Pagan soldiers to track, arrest, and capture one Joseph of Arimathea not more than six hours ago?"

Pilate's eyes glared unfettered rage at Annas as he continued to pace.

The wrinkled face of Annas turned ashen white.

Pilate continued. "Well, Annas, have you no answer?"

Caiaphas took a few steps toward Pilate, then stopped to look him dead in the eye. "Why are you making such an outrageous charge, governor? In front of your staff, your wife, and my friends? Is this why you called us here at this outrageous hour? To insult and berate us like misbehaving schoolchildren? Besides, what is your proof?"

He paused and took note of Annas who had just set himself carefully down on one of the couches, his eyes unfocused as though he were on the verge of losing consciousness.

Pilate roared with laughter and glanced at the others gathered there. His gaze fixed momentarily on his wife, Procula, then back to Caiaphas. "I love you patrician Jews of the Sanhedrin—always so high and mighty, pretending to be men of virtue, when in fact you're nothing but a brood of vipers. You really want me to lay out my proof for you—piece by piece, witness by witness?"

Annas shook his head, gazing down at the floor. "Son-in-law, at a time like this, it's been my experience that it's best to tell the truth. We've been caught. No sense pretending otherwise."

Pilate began strolling around the room, a huge grin on his face. "Now there's a novel concept—truth from a representative of the Sanhedrin family dynasty. What do you think, Caiaphas? Shall we venture further down this road to truth? Care to explain your plans of retribution against the man responsible for Jesus, the Nazarene, receiving a proper burial?"

Now it was Caiaphas who decided to find a seat, his face losing its color.

"Because, the way I see it, this is a blatant attempt by the ruling class of the Jewish elites to usurp Roman authority and sovereignty over all Judea. Caiaphas, would you agree that's what has actually taken place—in truth?"

Caiaphas grimaced and wiped his mouth. "Before I answer, your Excellency, is this meeting on or off the record?"

Pilate grinned ear-to-ear and began to nod knowingly. "Let's just say that, for the moment, we're off the record . . . unless I change my mind. So, what do you have to say for yourself, high priest of the Temple? Have you and your family broken Roman law?"

Caiaphas squirmed and stood. "Speaking off the record," he said, beginning to pace, "I can see where you might conclude that Roman law has been usurped. I'm not sure if the facts clearly establish that truth, but for the sake of reaching a conclusion to this off-the-record discussion, I'm willing pursue the question of what you, honorable governor, believe should happen next."

Pilate laughed and went to his wife, putting his arm around her shoulders. "Don't you just love it, Procula, when the high priest of the Temple gives the governor of Judea an answer like that? I mean, have you ever heard more high-density obfuscation in your life? These men proclaim to be men of faith, but in truth are more politician than I."

Procula smiled and looked adoringly at her husband, then whispered in his ear.

Pilate turned and faced all present. "It does occur to me that all of us have a problem—one that we would all do well to fix: A well-respected and honorable member of the Sanhedrin, namely Joseph of Arimathea, currently resides in a prison attached to the palace of the high priest of the Temple." He paused. "Would anyone like to dispute that truth?"

No one spoke.

"Before we proceed any further, I feel compelled to share some news relevant to Roman authority that just came to my attention by special messenger earlier last night. Sejanus has fallen from favor, and Tiberius has once again assumed the reins of power. As all of you well know, Tiberius hates unrest in any of his provinces, but especially in Judea."

The men of the Sanhedrin nodded their understanding.

"So now," Pilate continued, "with the priorities of Tiberius in mind, we come to the major issue that needs to be resolved: what are we going to do with Joseph of Arimathea?"

"Keep him in jail and let him starve to death?" Caiaphas suggested. "No one knows where he is and how he got there. In a matter of weeks, he'll be forgotten, along with the rest of the Jesus of Nazareth movement."

"Aaah, but that's where you're wrong, Mister High and Mighty Priest of the Temple," Pilate hissed at Caiaphas. "If that were the case, we wouldn't be here having this little chat—on or off the record. The Pagan soldiers that apprehended him were sloppy. Joseph's family knows where he is and how he got there—they witnessed the whole thing. And the word *will* spread among your people. Executing the Nazarene was meant to stop any Jewish unrest before it could be further agitated, but this could undo all that."

Annas cast a long look of disappointment at his son-in-law.

"Really, governor?" Caiaphas asked. "You know that for a fact?"

Pilate nodded. "Beyond any shadow of a doubt." Pilate turned to Procula. "Do you have something you'd like to say, my dear wife?"

Procula smiled and said, "I have it from a reliable source that Joseph has been planning to leave Jerusalem for months. I am also told that he intended to leave at the height of the Passover festivities and to make a new life for himself someplace in the west—possibly Gaul."

"And why would he want to do that?" Annas said.

Procula looked at Pilate, wondering if she should respond.

"Go ahead, dear wife, answer the man's question."

"According to my information," Procula said quietly, "he is exhausted from the politics of Jerusalem and its Temple. He's 49 years old, has plenty of money, and sees the whole political and religious situation in Judea crumbling by the day. Because of people like you, Caiaphas, he wants to take his family to a place of greater peace and tranquility—away from immediate conflict and potential bloodshed."

Caiaphas took a deep breath and addressed all those present.

"It seems to me—given what we've just heard—that Joseph would be only too happy to 'escape' from the prison he now occupies. We can certainly make sure he believes he is a wanted man and just let him sail off into the sunset, never to be heard from again. I don't see any problem with such a plan, provided, off course, it meets with the total approval of the governor and his staff."

Pilate looked around the room and hearing no objections from anyone, said, "This does meet with my approval." He then looked at his wife. "And remember, gentlemen of Jerusalem," he continued, "to avoid any possibility of future misunderstanding, this meeting, this conversation, and this conclusion never took place."

The men stood to leave.

"Oh, and Caiaphas," Pilate said. The whole Sanhedrin delegation turned to face the governor. "Never forget your place. I would hate for anything to happen to you or your family simply because you overreached. Am I understood?"

"Yes, lord governor."

"Good. Happy Sabbath to all of you."

Chapter Eight

Everyone gathered around Longinus. He had seemed so imposing, sitting atop his black stallion on Golgotha, commanding his soldiers to bring death to their Redeemer. Here, out of context, in civilian clothing with no helmet or storm or soldiers, they could see how nervous the tall, muscular young centurion was.

"*Ave Domina*," he said to Mother Mary. "I'm so very sorry if this is not what you were hoping for, but it's one of the things that Joseph said you asked for. Please accept my most profound apologies if what I've brought upsets you in any way."

With that, he handed the red cloth he'd been cradling in one arm to Mother Mary. As she opened the cloth, all could see that the centurion had brought the steel head of the lance used to puncture the dying heart of Jesus. Blood from Her Son had dried and covered at least half the head of the spear.

Mary's eyes swelled at the sight of the vile weapon and her Son's dried blood. Her face turned wan, lips nearly disappearing, as though having bitten into rotten fruit. Her hands shook as she looked up at the young Roman visitor. "Longinus, I thank you from the bottom of my heart for this blessed gift. It's... it's exactly what I asked for. For your great kindness, I pray that you will one day rest at peace in the presence of our Father in Heaven."

Longinus bowed his head as Mother Mary turned and walked toward her bedroom, kissing the dried blood on the steel head. "I need to be alone with my Son right now. What's left of Him."

No one else spoke.

John followed after Mother Mary to make sure she wasn't going to collapse or faint. He could not imagine what she was going through. The rest of Jesus' followers, John included, had only known Him for a few years before His murder and what they were feeling now—what John was feeling now—was worse than any heartbreak that had come before. To be Jesus' Mother... John just couldn't imagine.

Her head was on her pillow now, facing away from him, and clutching the lance head in its red cloth to her chest. John closed the bedroom door, but as soon as he took his hand off the door, Mother Mary's quiet, muffled sobbing leaked under the door and filled the large Upper Room.

"Have I done something wrong?" Longinus asked quietly.

"No," John said. "She really is thankful. But her Son was murdered in front of her. How did you think an object with His barely dried blood all over it was going to make her feel?"

Longinus looked at the floor, silent.

Mary Magdalene walked over to Longinus and whispered, "How would you like to do something truly helpful for all of us? You wouldn't have to do anything but stay here for a while and keep an eye out for anyone you think might be out to harm us? After all, for the moment, we're just a bunch of helpless women and a fisherman."

Longinus smiled. "It would be my honor. Where would you like me to set up?"

"Just outside, on the porch. You can see anyone coming up the steps, but they won't see you until you want them to."

Longinus nodded and moved outside.

Once the front door was shut, Mary Magdalene shook her head, the concern on her face visible in the dim light of dawn. She motioned for all present to gather around. Mary Clopas, Mary of Zebedee, her son the Apostle John, Martha of Bethany, Suzanne, and Joanna.

Magdalene continued in the faintest of whispers. "We have to discuss something extremely important, but we must keep it between us. Only us gathered here right now. Can we do that?"

Everyone nodded their agreement.

"I am... concerned for Mother Mary and her developing preoccupation with the blood and gore of her Son's death. Her watching almost at His side as He was systematically tortured and murdered by Roman executioners seems to have... well, she's been acting differently. We all see it. Like all of us, she's known for a long time that Her Son was going to have to die as part of His mission, but I think seeing the whole thing the way she did—up close, within arm's reach—it's left her in a state of torment for which I think she was unprepared.

"As I see it," she continued, "all of us and the Apostles have to do two things. One—bring comfort to Mother Mary and love Her with all our heart. And Two—get her back on track for the journey God left for Her—namely, to make sure all the Apostles feel loved and forgiven by God. Jesus taught forgiveness and that must begin with us, His followers. I know some of you are angry that many of those closest to Him went into hiding. I know if I were them, I would be angry with myself. But they must forgive themselves if they are to love themselves the way God loves them. And they must love themselves if they are to resume their mission—spreading Jesus' message of love."

She looked around at all the others. "Does anyone want to offer their own thoughts? Or disagree with me?"

Mary of Zebedee said, "I'm not sure I know what you're talking about. Aside from her kissing the head of the bloody lance, what else has she done that concerns you?"

Mary Magdalene nodded kindly. "You were not atop Golgotha with us, so let me tell you what I mean. First it was her insistence that Joseph and Nicodemus place the dead, and bloodied body of Jesus in her lap as soon as they removed Him from the cross; then it was her weird attempts to kiss Him as they carried Jesus' mutilated corpse to the burial site; then it was her frantic kisses all over the face of Jesus through the burial cloths while everyone was trying their best to properly bury Him before sunset—her kissing got so out of hand that Joseph and Nicodemus had to have her carried from the tomb and physically prevented from returning by your dear son John so the others could finish as best they could! We barely made it out before soldiers showed up to arrest any violations of our burial laws! And then there was her request that anything leftover from Golgotha be brought to her, no matter its condition or how much blood or flesh there was on it. And now, she's in her bed, clutching the point of that horrible spear and weeping as quietly as she can so we won't hear. It's heartbreaking."

No one spoke for a moment.

"Upon reflection," Mary of Zebedee said, "I think you're right. But I believe Mary's deep grief requires comfort from a peer. A peer in grief. An adult female with deep reserves of life experience. I love and admire my blessed son..." She smiled at John. "But you're still only a young man, John. Your life experiences are limited."

"I agree with that" Mary of Clopas said to Magdalene, "and I think you should be the one to assume that role. You have the life experiences and were right there every step of the way yesterday. And everyone knows her Son cared for you. You're practically family. If anyone can relate to Mother Mary's grief, it's you."

Mary Magdalene bowed her head and knelt. "I think we should all pray on this and ask the Father to show us His way as we all seek to be of comfort to His Son's Blessed Mother in this struggle. Let us pray for God to show us the path to best carry on Jesus' work alongside Mother Mary—especially in this, her incredibly burdened time of loss and anguish."

The others went to their knees, folded their hands, and joined Magdalene in silent prayer as tears ran slowly down all their respective faces.

Mother Mary could still be heard crying from her bedroom.

After several minutes, John stood. "I think it's time for me to go looking for as many of my fellow Apostles as I can find."

The others stood. Magdalena raised an eyebrow at John, as though she had known his thoughts earlier. "Are you certain you're ready to face them? After they fled?"

John nodded. "A grudge is a heavy thing. I do not intend to be weighed down when I offer my brothers my embrace. Besides, I'm no help here. Longinus can certainly do a better job of protecting this house than I could. And Mother... well, I think she does need a peer right now. She needs you. Not me."

Mary Magdalene nodded. "God's will be done. The quicker we can get all the other Apostles back here, the better for us all. Especially Mother Mary."

Martha of Bethany spoke up. "Why don't we go together, John? Your mother can come too. I'll bet at least some of the Apostles are at the family house in Bethany with Lazarus and sister Mary."

Once the three of them were out the door, Susanna and Joanna walked up to Mary Magdalene and pointed at the animal skin bags on the floor.

"Those hard balls of myrrh still need to be pulverized and made ready for the final burial on Sunday, right?" said Susanna.

"Yes," said Magdalene. "Are you volunteering? I know I'm wearing down after being out all night."

Joanna took a deep breath and said, "Actually, we were concerned about all the noise that it's going to take to get the job done. Mother Mary needs rest too, right?"

Magdalene twisted her mouth, deep in thought. "How about this?" she said. "Why don't you and Susanna go to Temple for awhile? You're right, it would be best to give Mother Mary some peace and quiet. God will provide a solution to our myrrh problem. A trip out into the city would also give you a chance to check in with your families and friends to see if any of the Apostles are hiding out with them."

"Good idea," Joanna said.

"Yes, I think that could work out well," said Susanna.

A few minutes later, after everyone had gone, Mary Magdalene was alone with the mid-morning light of the Sabbath. She got on her knees and began to pray.

Please, Father God, help me know what to do—help me know your path for me to best bring comfort and healing to Mother Mary. Seeing her flesh and blood, Your Son, so viciously beaten, tortured, and murdered, up close, all day long yesterday has badly scarred her body, mind, and spirit. What I'm asking for, dear Lord, is Your will for me to be of service and compassion and love to the Mother of Jesus. I really need Your help, dear Lord.

Just then, Magdalene heard Mother Mary's door open.

Thank you, dear God.

"Did I hear the front door open and close?" Mother Mary asked, weakly shuffling through her door. "What happened? Did someone else come to visit? Where are Peter, James, and Andrew?"

Magdalene rushed to the grieving woman's side. "It's alright,

Mary, I'm here." She quickly redirected Mary's steps back to the bed. Setting her back on the bed's surface, she knelt and gently hugged her dear friend. The cloth with Jesus' face on it lay on the floor with the bloody spear head.

"Where did everybody go?" Mary asked.

Magdalene covered the shivering woman with a blanket. "Everything is going to work out, Mary—you're not alone. All the others have gone to look for the Apostles or go to Temple. They'll all be back in a few hours. But I'm here with you, now, and I promise I'm not going anywhere. Oh, and," she paused for emphasis, "centurion Longinus has decided to stay and keep watch for anyone acting on Caiaphas' orders."

"You trust him?"

"You are the Mother to my Lord. I trust you."

Mary smirked, her eyes wet. "My Son often spoke of the difference between men who are kind and those who are nice. Nice men act out of a desire to be seen, no matter the cost; kind men act out of a desire to help, no matter the cost. Longinus strikes me as a man who is kind."

"You are very wise, Mother."

"My Son was wise."

"Your Son was kind." Magdalena glanced around the room. "Would you like some drinking water or wine? When did you last eat?"

Mother Mary yawned but shook her head. "Some water would be nice, but I just... I'd like your company for awhile. Sit with me, please. I... I think I need some help getting my bearings."

"Of course," Magdalena said, standing to fetch a skin of water.

"I just can't seem to push the murder of my Jesus out of my mind," Mother Mary said her voice echoing through the empty rooms "It still doesn't feel real. I keep expecting to wake up. Any second now, I think I'll wake up and all yesterday's memories will slip beyond my brains' reach as all dreams do. But I'm not waking up from yesterday, am I? My sweet Son, really was murdered before our eyes as if . . . "

As Magdalena returned with the water skin, Mother Mary took one of her friend's hands and squeezed it. "I don't know what I would have done without you, Mary. Thank you for being with me yesterday. Thank you for being with me now." She licked cracked dry lips and wiped her tear-streaked face. "You have been such a gift—you and John and my sister and Longinus—I can't thank you enough. Nicodemus and Joseph too. What would we have ever done without those God has sent to help us?"

She looked hard into Magdalene's eyes and began to nod. "We really do have to get all the right materials so we can bury my Son properly tomorrow, don't we?"

Magdalene nodded. "We already have everything here."

"Really?" Mary's eyes widened a moment before shutting for several seconds. With a deep sigh, she lay back down. "I'm afraid I don't have much strength left. I think I'm going to try to sleep one more time. I'll either wake up from this nightmare or I'll gather some of my strength back. There's so much to do..." Her voice trailed off.

Magdalene started to pull the covers up, but Mother Mary grabbed them and pulled them up herself. "Please, just sit here with me until I wake up. I'll be fine, one way or the other. Can you do that for me? Please?"

"Yes, I can do that, Mother," said Magdalene. "I promise."

BETHANY
THE HOME OF MARY, MARTHA, AND LAZARUS
MIDDAY OF THE SABBATH
33 AD
THE FIRST DAY

Peter, James, and Andrew had kept watch from the highest lookout points in Bethany since dawn on Friday. The three had run away when the Temple Jews started their trial against Jesus. They were expecting the Sanhedrin or the Romans to send men in search of anyone who might know the house where Jesus had stayed so often—the home of Mary, Martha, and Lazarus—and they had not had much sleep.

All the Apostles knew that the men of the Sanhedrin feared Jesus' message of radical love over the letter of the Law. They feared this not because they hated love—they didn't—but because if the letter of the Law was superseded, their power would be lost. The men of the Sanhedrin also deeply feared Lazarus. News of Lazarus' supposed return to life by Jesus' hand had flashed through the Passover crowds like wildfire. They didn't care whether the miracle had happened or not—a story repeated often enough becomes true for those who hear it. They only feared Lazarus' testimony to Jesus' divinity for the effect it would have on their own authority. Again, their fear was only for their own power.

Peter, James, and Andrew knew that they were always welcome at Lazarus' home. But as soon as Lazarus had begun talking about how Jesus raised him from death, none of these Apostles felt safe from the long reach of the men of the Sadducees. Apparently, neither did Lazarus, as he showed them several strategic places to post lookouts for Temple agents advancing in their direction. They also devised several plans to escape capture, depending on which pursuers came and from which direction.

These men had already heard the bloody rumors of how Jesus had been crucified, and that He had been buried in a tomb reserved for the aristocrats of Jerusalem, which was just absurd in their minds. A decent burial for Jesus could not have happened, they told each other. He had probably been burned to ashes along with the other criminals crucified that day. The Romans made it a point to advertise their policies for the disposition of crucified men, and there was no reason to expect anything different for Jesus.

So when James saw the Apostle John, his mother, and Martha hurrying down the stony road toward the family house—with no one in apparent pursuit—he leapt from his hiding place to intercept them.

"John! Martha! Mother!" he shouted. Without waiting for a reply, he wrapped his arms around each of their waists and hustled them into a safe cluster of trees where it would be hard for anyone to spot them. Turning to John, he said, "You were rushing down the path –is anyone following you?"

"No," the boy said, trying to catch his breath.

"Are you sure?" James asked.

"We took great precautions," Martha said.

"Good Lord, yes," added John's mother, hands on knees and panting. "We took so many different trails and back roads to get here, I'm almost dizzy from it all. Not even a hungry wolf could have followed us."

"So why were you running?" James continued. "Why are you in such a hurry?"

Lazarus, Mary of Bethany, and Peter approached, winded from their sprint to greet their sister and close friends.

"What are you doing here?" asked Peter. "Who sent you?"

"Mother Mary," said John. "She wants all of us back and together again with her."

James shook his head. "I don't believe she would say such a thing."

"Mother Mary?" Peter blurted, incredulously studying the three who had just arrived. "Why would she want us in her presence? Why would you? We ran from Jesus when He needed us most." He sniffed and let out a sad bark of shameful laughter. "He told me exactly what I would do before I did it. Exactly. And I had the arrogance to argue with Him, to argue that surely I, Peter, His friend, would never betray Him. And then He told me that I would do it before the cock crowed. I didn't even realize I had done it until I heard the crowing. But I did it. I betrayed Him. So why would His Mother want someone like me under the same roof as she?"

"That's all in the past, Peter" Martha said with kindness. "Mother Mary loves you. She forgives you. And she wants all of you to come back."

"How?" Peter fell to his knees and began to weep. "How can this possibly be? How could she ever forgive me? I may as well be Judas!"

"I was with Mother Mary when Jesus was killed," said John. "I saw everything she saw. Every time our Redeemer had His flesh ripped open by a Roman whip, I was there. When His cross dug into His shoulder and exposed His shoulder bone, I was there. When they hammered the metal spikes into His hands and feet, I was there. When He hung for hours trying His best not to suffocate under His own weight, I was there. When He was cold and had gone to His Father in Heaven and had to be carefully removed from His cross, I was there. Helping. Wondering why none of my brothers were there to help. But I know you, my three brothers. I know your heart. You're all good men. And I love you."

No one spoke for several moments as a breeze gently swept over them.

"And, I forgive you, Peter" John said at last, somewhat surprised that he actually meant it. "Please come back. None of us should be alone right now. And there is much to be done."

CHAPTER NINE

𝕿 he decision Susanna and Joanna made to go to Temple before checking in with their family and friends turned out to be quite fortunate for Joseph of Arimathea. When the two women arrived at Joanna's home, a message awaited them both under the governor's seal. It read: "Whenever you receive this, please rush to my private quarters. A personal issue demands your careful attention. You won't believe it."

It was signed by Procula Pilate.

One of the unexpected benefits of being the governor's wife in Jerusalem included an automatic welcome into the local elite society, Judeans and Romans alike. Because of her youthful good-looks and witty conversational skills, Procula quickly became a favorite at local aristocratic social events and became part of the same group of elite friends and associates as Joanna and Susanna.

During the time they had been friends, their conversations with Procula had inevitably led to the subject of Jesus and His message of unconditional love. The two life-long friends found a willing listener in the governor's wife, and they soon became close. Thus, it wasn't a complete surprise that Procula would send a secret message to Joanna and Susanna, but the final sentence caught their attention.

"You won't believe it?" they whispered to each other while they hurried toward Procula's private quarters. The entirety of the past week had been nothing short of unbelievable.

One of Procula's trusted servants recognized Joanna and Susanna upon their arrival and showed them both directly to Procula's personal suite.

"Thank you, Rebecca," Procula said to her servant as they entered. "That will be all for the moment, but please get some rest out of earshot. We have a long night ahead."

After a warm welcome, the hostess asked them to sit and make themselves comfortable. "I sent my servant out of eavesdropping range for a reason," she began in a low voice. "What I'm about to tell you is top-secret and potentially dangerous. But, please hear me out."

Joanna and Susanna looked at each other and shrugged. "You have our attention," Joanna said.

Procula took a deep breath. "Did either of you know that Joseph of Arimathea has been arrested and is currently incarcerated in the prison of the Temple Guards?"

"No, we did not!" Susanna said, taken aback.

"How can that be?" said Joanna. "He's a member of the Sanhedrin and a man of wealth! Joseph is greatly respected throughout all Jerusalem. Who would do such a crazy thing? He's the most law-abiding man I know!"

After a moment, Susanna said, "Wait, don't tell me. Caiaphas?"

"The whole family," replied Procula, her eyes wide and eyebrows raised.

"Well," said Joanna, "you were half-right. "I didn't believe it. But if Joseph has been arrested, I certainly believe Caiaphas and

Annas were behind it. Does Joseph's family know about it?"

"Indeed," Procula said. "They witnessed the whole thing. Pagan soldiers under Caiaphas' orders. And that's the problem."

"Problem?" Susanna echoed.

"Here's where everything gets tricky," Procula continued. "My husband knows about it and wants it completely forgotten. Caiaphas knows he overstepped but has put forth the notion that he and his family would prefer that Joseph just escape so they can pretend the whole thing never happened."

"And what about Joseph's family?" Joanna said.

"They just want him free. After that, they're happy with whatever Joseph decides to do next, given the events of these past few days."

"So why is an escape in and of itself necessary?" said Joanna. "Why can't your husband just unlock the prison and let him go?"

"Because even though Caiaphas overstepped his authority, he was enacting the will of the Sanhedrin. They hoped to make an example out of Joseph for allowing Jesus to be buried in the Arimathea family tomb, thus embarrassing the Sanhedrin leadership."

"Why would that embarrass them?" asked Susanna.

"Because Jesus is not related to Joseph in any way."

Joanna and Susanna scowled and nodded understandingly.

The Sanhedrin had Jesus executed in the most humiliating way possible so as to show all Judeans what happens when someone claims to be King of the Jews. Such words carry great power. Such a title given to Jesus undermines the Sanhedrin's authority among its own people. By burying Jesus in the Arimathea tomb, Joseph symbolically sided with your friend and spat in the faces of his peers."

"So why are you sharing this with us?" asked Susanna.

"Because each second Joseph stays imprisoned is another chance for Caiaphas to pay off a guard to murder him. Now, I have a plan for Joseph's escape, but before I share those specific details, are you willing to help? It could be quite dangerous."

Joanna and Susanna looked at each other and took a deep breath. "Yes, but we need more particulars," said Joanna. "What makes it dangerous?"

"Because you would be taking complete responsibility for it. Politics dictate that neither myself nor the governor can have any connection to this plan or its execution. If anything goes wrong and you are caught, we will swear ignorance by all the gods that ever were."

Procula stopped and studied her two friends.

Susanna took a deep breath, "I'm in, as long as your plan makes any sense. Any chance to stick it to those pious hypocritical dogs."

Joanna smiled. "Oh alright. Now that you've got us both jumping out of the water at your bait, tell us your plan. It's you, so I expect nothing short of sheer madness."

"Just you wait. First, let's start with time involved: it's probably going to take most of tonight. Can both of you commit that much time away from your family and friends on the Sabbath? I can cover for you if you need an alibi—you know, us girls have a lot to talk about."

Susanna giggled. "Don't we always?"

JERUSALEM
UPPER ROOM
SUNSET OF THE SABBATH
33 AD
THE FIRST DAY

Mary Magdalene had been sitting in silence with Mother Mary all afternoon and was beginning to agonize that something might have happened to her friends. She worried most about Martha, John, and his mother. Maybe Caiaphas had directed some of his thugs to hide near the home of Lazarus so they could seize them all, once they showed up.

It also concerned her that so much had yet to be done in order to be ready to finish burying Jesus. They would have to be completely ready with everything at first light—only twelve hours from now. The fact that Mother Mary still needed more deep sleep before she could embrace her responsibilities as the comforting Mother of the crucified Nazarene caused Magdalena no small additional distress.

Dear Father in Heaven, please help. There's so much that needs to be done, and I don't know what I should do or say to help make it happen. I know I should stop worrying and surrender to Your love and will. Please help me stop being fearful.

Just then she heard voices and the sound of footsteps climbing stairs to the Upper Room.

Thank you, God. I pray they're all safe.

Magdalena heard John whispering just outside. "Mother Mary's probably sleeping." he said. The front door unlocked and slowly swung upon. On his way in, John nodded approval at Longinus, who had not moved from his post all day.

"Praise God," said Martha, once inside. "Looks like Mother is still sleeping."

Mary Magdalene quietly closed the door to Mother Mary's room and went to greet John and the others. Her chest warmed at the sight of everyone's faces. The Room was full with Jesus' followers—Peter, John, James, Thomas, Lazarus, Mary, Martha, Mary of Clopas, Mary of Zebedee, and Andrew. Everyone began hugging, tears on most every cheek.

Mary of Clopas shared with Magdalene that she had talked with Susanna and Joanna at Temple, but they were going to stop at their homes before returning to the Cenacle. Mary's sister had also found young Andrew at Temple and brought him back with her. The two had caught sight of those walking with John and James and joined them before arriving at the foot of the stairs to the Upper Room.

No one reported being challenged or mistreated by Romans or Temple Guards.

"I think there are just too many people on the streets," said Peter by way of explanation. "Anyone trying to start trouble with us would probably risk starting a riot. We still have a lot of support amongst the people."

"That's why they held His trials at night," said John. "To avoid possible civil unrest."

Magdalena could hear it in John's voice—he still had not slept.

"Hey John," she whispered. "Would you mind staying in Mother Mary's room for a little so I can organize the work for Jesus' re-burial tomorrow?"

John looked almost insulted at first, but yawned and agreed without needing much convincing, closing Mother Mary's door behind him without a sound.

Under Magdalena's instruction, the others began the work of preparing for the final burial and started moving the materials down the stairs onto the walkway below so that the noise of pulverizing the myrrh would have less chance of awakening Mother Mary.

Peter and Andrew decided that they needed to organize and clean-up the Supper Room, in case it might be needed with so many people present and more on the way. Still, Peter felt useless and out of sorts, but couldn't think what else he should be doing. Finally, he said to Andrew, "Why are we doing this? It's just busy work. Shouldn't we be helping the others?"

Andrew picked up a blanket and began folding it. "Don't you

remember? Jesus told us to straighten this place up as He was leaving night before last? There must be a reason."

"Yes, I remember. He said a lot of other things too."

"What does that have to do with cleaning up?"

Peter gazed out the front door and into the bustling city for a brief moment. "Nothing really. I just can't stop thinking about what a weak person I am. I ran away when my friend needed me most!"

"Enough of this self-pity, brother. Pull yourself together. We need you to be yourself—you know, the same loud-mouth, self-assured pain-in-the-neck Peter."

The two brothers exchanged a quick knowing smirk.

Peter picked up a blanket and tossed it into one of the dark corners. "I can't help it." He turned back to the window, where he could avoid looking any of them in the eye. "I keep thinking of Jesus asking me to stay awake with Him in the garden and His telling me that I needed to stop my prideful ways and that I would soon disown Him three times before the cock crowed. And it all happened . . . "

With those words, tears broke through and flowed down his face.

Mary Magdalene had been standing in a corner nearby. She walked soundlessly to Andrew and motioned for him to go help the others downstairs.

Peter kept sobbing.

She cleared her throat and waited for him to look up. Finally he did.

"So, Peter," she said, "I guess you're beyond all hope. You made some mistakes, so now you're useless. Nobody can count on you to keep your word, so you might as well just go back to fishing for the rest of your life and forget all about doing God's work."

He nodded. "That's exactly right," he said, gasping and trying to get himself under control. "Doing God's work? What a colossal joke! I'm barely qualified to put on my own sandals."

"Oh stop it!" she hissed. "You're better than this. Feeling sorry for yourself is not who you are. Jesus would never have picked you if he thought you were a quitter or a whiner."

Peter shook his head. "Cowardly windbag—that's me!"

"No you're not. You're just so full of yourself that you think you're the only person in the world who's ever gone back on a promise. What are you thinking? That you've committed a sin so big that God cannot possibly forgive you? That's the enemy talking. God forgives all of us. Jesus, the man you're beating yourself up over, taught us all that unconditional love starts with forgiveness. Is that hard for you?"

Peter ran muscular fingers through his thick long hair before easing his large overweight body onto the hardwood. "I'm not sure what's too hard for me right this moment." He took a deep breath. "I feel overwhelmed by everything—deciding when to eat is probably all I could handle at the moment."

"When did you eat last?"

"While we were walking from Bethany, I had some fruit."

"When did you last have a decent sleep?"

"I don't know—probably not since early Thursday."

"So you're probably the only one in that situation. God's probably punishing you."

Reluctantly, Peter let out a small laugh.

Magdalena smiled at him. "The best thing you can do right now is to go find a quiet place and take a quick nap. I think that's what you need more than anything. Mother Mary is sleeping right now too, but I know she wants to talk with you—but only if you can stop whining."

Peter tried to smile at Magdalene, but his eyes glazed over from mental and physical exhaustion. "You're probably right," he said in a whisper, crumpling to the floor and crawling toward the corner where he had tossed the blanket a minute ago. "Sleep sounds like the best idea I've heard all day."

✦

JERUSALEM
TEMPLE GUARD PRISON
JOSEPH OF ARIMATHEA'S CELL
THIRD WATCH
33 AD
THE FIRST DAY

For Susanna and Joanna, the escape plan that Procula presented seemed like it had decent odds of success, provided they could locate the people they needed on such short notice.

"Just show up at the Temple prison with a large group of family and friends dressed as if they were coming from an end-of-Passover party for your influential old-money friends, neighbors, and sycophants," instructed Procula.

"If soldiers demand to know why we're all there?" Susanna asked.

"Tell the truth," said Procula. "Or half of it, anyway. Say you're there to bring some holiday cheer to your dear friend and associate, the honorable Joseph of Arimathea. If they press you, tell the prison guards that you and your influential friends plan to leave no stone unturned to legally get Joseph set free because he had done so much to help the people of the city and all Judea."

"Oh, so this is a mission of moral support for a dear friend and humanitarian?" said Joanna.

"Precisely," Procula said, taking a deep drink of wine. "And with such a large crowd of influential friends, it would be truly terrible if things got ugly. Wouldn't want any civil unrest in the streets,

97

would we?"

Joanna and Susann originally thought the hardest part of the plan would be finding enough male friends as tall as Joseph on such short notice—especially men who would be willing to get involved in this insane scheme. But since Joseph enjoyed such high regard throughout the region, Susanna and Joanna actually had to reassign several men who volunteered to help with Procula's plan.

Susanna and Joanna chose two tall, muscular men to provide physical support for "an ailing deaf-mute cripple"— a dummy whose face and hair would be concealed by a head-wrapping. This "man" was to be an essential member of the escape entourage—Joseph's dying twin brother Amittai, if anyone asked. The women made sure that he perfectly matched the height, build, and hair color of Joseph.

Subsequent to the early morning non-meeting at the Pilate residence, word was passed to Chief Chuza to make sure his guards knew that they should expect a visit from Joseph's family and friends at almost any hour. "These people are to be received with the utmost courtesy, regard, and consideration and granted full access to the prisoner, Joseph of Arimathea," read the written orders to his men. "Bear in mind that this prisoner is a prominent and respected member of the Sanhedrin, and that he and his visitors should be treated with the highest regard at all times."

The escape team assembled at the Temple Guard Prison around midnight. Joseph's oldest son, David, acted as their spokesman.

"Good evening, Sergeant of the Guard," David said, standing at the entrance to the prison." The other people Joanna and Susanna had recruited stood behind him. "My name is David of Arimathea." He handed the guard his identification documents. "I'm here with family and friends to pay a visit to your prisoner, Joseph of Arimathea."

The Corrections Officer scowled and studied the credentials in his lamplight. "Kind of late, isn't it?"

"Yes, Sergeant, it is, but a number of us have to leave the city in just a few hours and make long return trips to our homes, now that the Sabbath is over. Some of us have hundreds of miles to cover."

"I see," said the guard, squinting out into the darkness at those lined up behind David. "But I see from your papers that you live here in Jerusalem. So, why are *you* here at this hour?"

"He's my father. We're all here to give him moral support on one of our most sacred holidays until we can legally get him out of prison to resume his duties with the Sanhedrin."

The guard scratched his head for a moment and fingered through some documents on his desk. "Your father is a member of the Sanhedrin?" He studied several papyrus scrolls. "And his name is Joseph of Arimathea? Is that right?"

"Yes, Sergeant, that's correct."

"I'm sorry, sir," the guard said, "I've been on duty all day, and my brain is a little sleepy. I apologize if I've caused you any distress." He carefully studied one document. "How many did you say you have with you?"

"We're a total of twelve," David said. "Would you like to see their documents?"

"No, I have everything I need right here, sir. I know who you are and where to find you if I have any questions. Give me just a second. I'll make sure the other guards don't create any problems for you."

He started to walk back into the prison, remembered something, and came back. "How long do you expect to be here?"

David shrugged. "No more than an hour or so."

The guard nodded and left to talk with his associates.

Susanna and Joanna looked at each in the dark. "Say a little prayer he doesn't change his mind," Joanna whispered. "I don't trust him."

"Don't worry," said one of the two large servants guarding the "cripple twin." "We know what to do if he does."

A few minutes later, the entrance guard returned. "Everything is ready. All of you may now proceed inside the prison compound, after me. Stay close together in single file and walk in the middle of each corridor, especially the women. Remember, the men in here are mostly killers or worse. If they get their hands on any of you, you'll probably be dead or badly injured before I could come to your aid."

The guard had a large torch that he carried high in the air so everyone could see. Another guard came and took the first guard's place at the front gate.

No one spoke.

The moment the gate guard and the others entered the prison, the inmates began shouting, yelling expletives, and screaming vulgarities.

Immediately behind the guard and David came Joanna and Susanna, followed by the two body guard servants, carrying the deaf-mute between them. The remaining women and tall men followed closely as best they could. There wasn't much light at the back of the column.

Joanna and Susanna turned and whispered to each other in the dimness.

"Hope these steel bars can hold these men. I think if they pushed at the same time, all the bars would fall on us," said Joanna.

"You're always so cheerful at a time like this!" said Susanna.

The raucous din continued for about five minutes until the visitor column came to a part of the prison where there were no other inmates—just empty cells. Shortly thereafter, the guard stopped and asked David to hold the torch while he unlocked the cell. Having done so, he took the torch back from David and entered the cell.

David's father had been asleep and turned, squinting at the sudden glare of light.

"I've brought you some visitors, Joseph," announced the guard as he lit a torch that had been hanging dormant on the wall.

With that, their escort stepped to one side and allowed David and the others to enter the cold, damp cell. Once the visitors were all inside, the guard closed the steel gate and locked it.

"I won't be far away," he said. "Just call 'Guard' when you're ready to leave."

The visitors all remained silent as the guard walked away. The cell was cramped, but the sheer number of bodies would work to their advantage.

"Alright," Joanna whispered. "It's time."

CHAPTER TEN

JERUSALEM
UPPER ROOM
DUSK OF THE SABBATH
33 AD
THE FIRST DAY

other Mary turned in her sleep and opened one eye. Seeing John sitting beside her, eyes closed, she opened both eyes and sat up. "Where is everyone?" she muttered to herself, squinting.

"They're downstairs," John said, blinking himself awake. "Preparing for the final burial at dawn."

"Who's here?"

John listed the names of those who had come back.

"What about Susanna and Joanna?"

"I don't know where they are. They went to Temple and were going to stop at their homes before returning."

"Well, when they come back, please let me know. I want to ask them something." Mary wiped her caked and bloodshot eyes. "And would you please bring me some water? I'm really quite thirsty."

"Of course, Mother."

"Oh, and John? While you're out there, tell Peter I want to speak with him."

John nodded and left her bedroom, returning moments later holding a small clay jar of water, Peter following close behind.

"Thank you, John," she said, taking the water. She motioned for Peter to close the door once John had left.

Peter returned to her bedside.

"Sit, sit," she said, studying the distressed Apostle between sips.

Peter sat down and ran both hands through his oily hair, squirming in the chair, and bouncing one leg. He kept his eyes focused on the floor, refusing to look her in the eye.

"Peter," she began, "you look terrible."

He nodded. "I know."

"Why won't you look me in the eye?"

He continued staring at the floor.

"Why are you afraid to look me in the eye?"

He didn't answer at first as tears began to slide down his cheeks and into his thick salt and pepper beard. "Because I feel guilty . . . and useless and ashamed and cowardly. . . and I don't know what to do except to say how truly sorry I am and to . . . to beg, humbly, for your forgiveness."

"Of course you're forgiven; you don't need to beg for it. My Son taught you better than that. But what about you?"

He looked up at her face for the first time since entering the room. "What do you mean?"

"Can you forgive yourself?"

Peter doubled over, weeping uncontrollably now, his head resting on his own thigh. "How can I do that? What I did was unforgiveable!"

Mother Mary turned in the bed, pushed back her bedclothes, and started to stand.

Peter stopped her. "You need to stay in bed, Mother," he said, wiping his eyes. "You're in no condition to stand."

She smiled at him. "What are you talking about? I want to give you a hug so you'll know I truly forgive you and that I still love you, just as my Son did. But now you're not going to let me hug you?"

"Apologies! Of course you can hug me. I would love for you to hug me, but I don't feel worthy of such a gift. I abandoned your Son—the man I proclaimed to love—in His time of need. How can you possibly want to hug me?"

"I want to hug you because I love you and my Son loves you. He loves us all—especially when we do things we're ashamed of."

Peter stood and bent over Mother Mary's bed, embracing her and sobbing into her shoulder.

"Thank you for loving me and my Son," she said. "Now sit down, there's something I need for you to see. I'm hoping it will help bring you as much peace and comfort as it has me." She reached under her pillow and pulled out the white cloth with the smiling and un-bloodied face of Jesus on it. "See this?"

Peter went cross-eyed. "What is that?" He gasped when he finally saw it. "Oh my Father in Heaven. Where did it come from?"

"A girl named Veronica came here early on the Sabbath and gave it to me," she said, her eyes wet above her beaming smile. "She got it from Jesus while he was carrying the cross."

Peter stared wide-eyed at the clear imprint of Jesus' face. The face of his friend. The face of the man he loved, then abandoned.

"I can't do this," he said, bolting up, stammering for the right words. "There's no possible way I can do this." he said, swinging the door open.

"Peter!" Mother Mary exclaimed. "We haven't finished our talk."

Peter walked out through the swinging door, barreling through the Upper Room and out the front door.

John hurried into Mother's bedroom. "Are you okay?"

"No. I'm trying to do the right things, to say the right things. But I feel like it's all coming out wrong. Honestly, John, I don't know if I'll ever be okay again."

104

JERUSALEM
TEMPLE GUARD PRISON
JOSEPH OF ARIMATHEA'S CELL
THIRD WATCH
33 AD
THE FIRST DAY

"Father," David whispered to Joseph, "are you alright? Did they hurt you?"

Joseph shielded his eyes from the glare of the flickering torch. "Yes, I'm well enough, they just don't let me sleep. But what are you doing here? Especially at this time of night?" He looked around at all those in the cell. "And why are there so many of you?"

"That's a long story, Father," David said with a smirk. "One we expect you'll want to listen to very carefully."

"What do you mean? It's past midnight and you come busting in here with all these people and now you want to tell me a story? The only story I want to hear is what you're doing to get me out of here?"

David, Susanna, and Joanna exchanged glances and grins.

"What's so funny?" Joseph said. "These people mean to hold me here forever and stop bringing me food and water. They want me to starve to death."

"Who told you that?" David said.

"Those soldiers who arrested and brought me here. They work for Caiaphas and Annas."

David looked in the direction of the cell door and listened for a moment.

"Does anyone hear anyone coming?" asked Susanna.

Those standing by the gate door shook their heads "no."

"We have to speak quietly and quickly," whispered Joanna. "We're here to break you out of this prison, right now. But we need your total cooperation and your willingness to do what we ask, even if it seems nonsensical. Are you willing to do that?"

Wide-eyed, Joseph said, "Yes, I think so."

"First, we've all got to start singing," whispered Susanna, "as if we're celebrating the end of Sabbath. Everyone in here—including you Joseph—has to start singing now, not loudly, just softly and reverently. And the singing has got to be continuous" She looked at the tall people against the cell gate. "You people especially."

Everyone in the cell began to sing.

"I take it that's all a distraction." Joseph scowled. "What are we really doing?"

"Switching you for the fake person your two servants brought in," Joanna said.

"And how are we going to do that?"

"Father," David said, "don't ask so many questions. Just take off your outer clothes. We're going to put the clothes on you that the dummy has on and your clothes on him."

"And then what?"

"We're going to walk out of here with your two favorite servants holding you, like you were a dummy." said Susanna. "Or like your deaf-mute identical twin brother."

"Then we leave the real dummy here," said Joanna, "under the covers and sound asleep from our comforting singing."

"Just like you were when we first came in."

Joseph smiled at them and nodded. "Alright. Do you think it'll work?"

"Probably," said David. "But only if you take your clothes off and stop asking so many questions."

"Okay, okay," the older man said and began singing along with the others.

It took several minutes for David, Joanna, Susanna, the two servants, and Joseph working together to manage the switch of clothes and to pose the hastily assembled dummy in the cot, facing the rear stone wall as if asleep, exactly as Joseph had been when his visitors arrived.

The soft and reverent singing never stopped. No one cared if they were on key. Finally all their tasks had been accomplished.

David looked around the cell and at Susanna and Joanna. "Are we ready?" he asked.

Susanna and Joanna nodded.

"Call the guard," Joseph said at last. "I'm ready." He looked to either side at his faithful servants. "You know what to do, if they stop us?"

"Indeed," came the immediate response from his faithful servants.

"Guard?" David called out.

JERUSALEM
THE CENACLE
SUNDAY PRE-DAWN
33 AD
THE FIRST DAY

Mary Magdalene couldn't believe her eyes. Perhaps her lack of sleep was making her more easily impressed, but she hadn't been holding her breath for such an outcome to the day.

Everyone except Mother Mary and John had put their personal feelings aside and worked all night. John spent most of the night at Mother's side—as Magdalene had requested—to make sure the older woman would not be disturbed and could receive the sleep she needed to regain her ability to function. But eventually young John came to Magdalene, requesting that someone else take his place. He hadn't had any sleep either. Mary Clopas, who for some reason had awakened on her own, gladly volunteered to take John's place for a few hours.

Magdalene had sent Longinus home during Third Watch—the Lord well knew the invaluable services he had contributed to their efforts.

Despite their grief and trauma, everyone at the Cenacle had worked as a team and the 100 pounds of myrrh, fresh linens, and aloes for the proper burial of Jesus lay fully prepared on the Upper Room floor.

The logistics for getting these necessities to the tomb of their beloved teacher and friend had not been finalized. How could they possibly transport in broad daylight all these burial essentials without inviting unwanted attention? Now that the Sabbath was over, Caiaphas and the Romans would likely be lying in wait for anyone associated with Jesus.

And what about the Roman guards that Caiaphas had posted to watch the tomb? Did those soldiers stay the whole night? Would someone come to take their place? If so, would they try to prevent Magdalene and her friends from reopening the tomb to administer the final burial procedures under Jewish Law?

She needed more information. She would need to go out into the remaining hours of darkness and take a close look at what was going on at the tomb. If the guards were still there, she was going to need a lot more people to be able to deal with those three sentries. She suddenly regretted sending Longinus home—but he, too, had been beyond exhaustion.

Yes, she was tired. This was the third night she had been without sleep. But for right now, she needed to hurry to the tomb and back lest the dawn steal her last chance to move unnoticed through the streets of the city. She wrapped her head and quietly slipped out the front door of the Upper Room.

It was still pitch dark outside.

JERUSALEM
TEMPLE GUARD PRISON
JOSEPH OF ARIMATHEA'S CELL
FOURTH WATCH
33 AD
THE FIRST DAY

No sooner had David called out, when the front gate guard came hustling up the corridor, torch held high. "Sorry, I took so long," he said. "You didn't use all your time."

The moment he stopped by the cell door to open it, David, Susanna, and Joanna put a finger to their lips and whispered, "Shhh..."

The guard scowled. "What's the matter?" He unlocked the cell door and stepped aside for all the visitors to walk out.

As the guard re-locked the cell, David stood beside him, shaking his head in frustration. "You know," he said to the guard. "You just can't plan for some things. We came all this way, brought all these people—even his twin brother from Rome—and he just can't stop his eyes from closing. We ended up dousing the torch pretty quick. I'm telling you, old age hits everyone differently, my friend. Anyway, we'll be back this afternoon after he's had a chance to get some decent rest."

"That's against the rules, you know," said the guard.

"It is?" said David. "It was never our intent to cause any trouble, we're just very worried about my father's health. Those soldiers who brought him in here apparently knocked him around pretty good. Perhaps tomorrow instead?"

"Yeah. Sorry to hear he got roughed up on the way in," said the guard. "I didn't know anything about him until I came to work. There he was—no explanation, just a note telling us his name and that he's a member of the Sanhedrin, but no reason for why he's in here."

The guard led the entourage single file toward the front gate in silence the rest of the way. By now most of the other inmates were either in bed, almost asleep, or fully comatose. When the escape party finally reached the front gate, the gate guard returned the documents David had provided, and said, "Sorry for your father being so tired. I guess we'll see you tomorrow."

As they were filing out, the second guard came up and looked over the whole group. "So who's this guy that's being carried by those two big men? Why'd you bring that man in here?"

David took another deep breath. "He's Joseph's twin brother, visiting from Rome. He's deaf and dumb and crippled from a hunting accident. He and Joseph are twins and haven't seen each other in years."

"I see," said the second guard, walking closer to Joseph and his two servants. "Sure got him bundled up enough; he should be sweating." With that he grabbed one end of the garment covering Joseph's face and flipped it so his whole face became exposed.

Joseph didn't flinch, eyes closed, not a muscle moving.

"What are you doing?" shouted David. "He's an invalid."

"Oh yeah?" said the second guard and slapped Joseph in the face.

Joseph moaned like a caged animal.

"What is the meaning of this?" yelled David, while the women grabbed each other in fear.

"I think I want to go back to the cell. Check if your dad's really sleeping or not. This whole thing looks fishy to me."

Once the second guard had taken one step toward the rear of

the prison, one of Joseph's massive servants grabbed him by the throat and lifted him up over his head. As he glared into the eyes of the guard mere inches from his face, he growled through clenched teeth, "You really don't want to go all the way back there and wake him up, do you? There's an awful lot of us who came out tonight to see him. You wouldn't want any unrest among so many citizens over your treatment of respected members of Sanhedrin, would you?"

The guard gagged and turned blue in the face as Joseph's servant slowly lowered him to the ground. When the guard finally landed, he began coughing and choking, then lost his footing and fell to the ground.

"Nope," said the gate guard. "I don't think he wants to go back and wake up your father." Everyone turned to look at this guard. "Sorry about this man's poor manners. He's new. Still has a lot to learn. On behalf of all the guards at this prison, please accept my humble apology for this entire incident. I will make it my personal mission to make sure that your father's rest is not disturbed for any reason. You have my word on that."

David had not yet recovered from his shock at what had just taken place. Finally, he said, "Thank you very much, officer. We appreciate your willingness to keep an eye out for my father. And we certainly hope that this other guard has learned a valuable lesson."

With that, David turned to his companions. "Let's go home. I could use some sleep myself." Looking at the gate guard, he said, "We'll probably be back tomorrow afternoon."

When they had walked far enough away so that they were out of sight from the prison, the two servants lowered Joseph onto his own feet.

"Well, that was a close call," the older man said. He patted both his servants on the back. "Many thanks for all your help. Lifting that guard up by the throat was a touch of brilliance. And you two," he said to Susanna and Joanna. "You dreamed up the perfect jail break on very short notice. Thank you. I'm forever in your debt."

"We were glad to be of help," Susanna said.

"You were pretty brilliant yourself, Father," said David. "When that guard slapped you in the face, I thought you might try to hurt him."

"Oh, I wanted to," Joseph said. "Thank you, dear God, for your incredible help in stopping me from hurting that rude man." Turning to Susanna and Joanna he said, "Before I forget it, I've got that tunic Jesus wore saved at my house for Mother Mary. I'll have it brought to you as soon as possible, but I'll be out of town before long."

The two women looked at each other, puzzled.

"I've been planning this move for some time. This whole incident with Caiaphas and his thugs just sped up the process. I'm a wanted man now."

"Goodness," said Joanna, "When are you leaving?"

"As soon as we can get to Joppa and on a ship for anywhere in Europe."

David scowled. "I don't know how we can get that tunic to Joanna or Susanna. I just grabbed everything you left at the house, Father, and packed it up. I'm guessing the tunic is in there somewhere, but I'm not going to try and find it today."

Joseph sighed and shook his head. "Well, I take it all back, ladies. We'll have to ship it to you once we get to Joppa. Please give Mother Mary my sincerest apologies for the hastiness of our family. I'm sure Jesus' tunic would greatly help ease her sorrow if she could only have it today, but it seems as though it wasn't meant to be."

"Dad, I'll try to find a quicker solution. Right now, we need to be on our way!"

"What an incredible woman—that wonderful mother of Jesus,"

Joseph said, deep in thought. "And Mary Magdalene, she's pretty amazing herself. Always thinking. Always in motion. She was there the whole time, wasn't she? On Golgotha?"

"Yes she was," said Joanna. "Every horrible step of the way."

"That can't have been easy for her. I pray her strength continues to hold."

Chapter Eleven

Jerusalem
Jesus' Tomb
Sunday Dawn
33 AD
The First Day

ary Magdalene's lack of sleep was starting to affect her. She was making mistakes. She miscalculated how far it was from the Cenacle to the Arimathea tomb. How long had she been walking? It felt like hours. When she had last departed this garden with Joseph of Arimathea, Nicodemus, Mother Mary, and the others, the length of the trip never registered in her memory. Was that just yesterday? The day before? Day and night had all begun to blur together. Everything felt like a fearful nightmare.

Winding through a maze of dead-end streets, Magdalene had to hurry from the Upper Room northward, up dark narrow roads and alleys toward the tomb. Although her journey actually only covered a mile or so in actual distance, the potential danger around every dark corner made it seem longer—she was, she had to remind herself, a woman very much alone in a potentially lethal situation. Dressed in black head to toe, she scurried carefully between shadows, taking care to note the slightest movement of any other pedestrians. She thought of how blessed she had been the last time she ventured out into the darkness of Jerusalem by herself and gave thanks. God had truly sent Longinus to keep her safe.

Eventually she arrived at the garden where Jesus' tomb had been sculpted out of a gigantic wall of rock for the family of Joseph of Arimathea. Since Magdalene had already been to His sepulcher, she already had a good idea of how to conceal herself from the Roman soldiers sent by Pilate and the Sanhedrin to make sure no one entered the tomb.

But, were her eyes deceiving her? The Roman soldiers seemed to have abandoned their post. Magdalene took particular care in making sure that the soldiers weren't hiding someplace nearby, waiting to arrest anyone who showed up at the tomb. As she inched her way closer to the sepulcher, she could see that the huge circular stone that had been sealed in place by the soldiers now stood in its original position to the right of the tomb's opening. From what she could see, someone had broken into the tomb. It was empty.

This could mean only one thing: Jesus had been stolen from His tomb. Magdalene began to cry. She turned and burst into a sprint heading back to the Cenacle House.

Why? she thought, over and over *Why?* She had no room in her head for any other thoughts as she bound up the stairs to the Upper Room.

"They've taken Jesus," she blurted at the top of her lungs. "Somebody's taken Jesus from His tomb."

"What are you talking about?" said Peter, his mouth agape. He felt better now that he'd had a chance to catch up on much needed sleep, but nothing had prepared him for this news.

Magdalene wiped sweat from her forehead and tried to catch her breath. "The tomb is open," she said. "The Roman guards are gone. So is Jesus."

John scratched his head. "You've just come from there?"

She nodded, still catching her breath.

"The Roman guards are gone, and the tomb is open . . . and

empty?" John asked.

"Yes."

"Roman guards?" asked Peter. "What Roman guards?"

"You weren't there. I'll explain on the way," John said. "Come on. If someone has really stolen Jesus' body, it could be the work of the Sanhedrin!"

They both bounded down the stairs, John leading the way and Peter close behind. There it was again—a reminder of his unexplained absence from his friends when he was needed most.

Magdalene, although not recovered from her return run, hurried down the stairs after them, her thoughts racing. Perhaps it was the Romans who had taken him—but then what would they do with His body? Maybe they planned to further mock and ridicule His body? What more could they want with Him? He was dead! What further victory over Jesus' movement could the Jewish leaders possibly hope for?

She ran as best she could but the trip somehow seemed even longer this time. She just wanted to lay down. She wanted all of this to be over.

By the time she arrived back at the tomb, Peter and John were outside, looking around. Peter took a step inside, and John remained outside, peering in.

Magdalene ran up to where Peter stood.

"He's definitely gone," the older Apostle said. "The linen burial cloths are here though—set down in separate places."

John entered the tomb and looked around. "Look how the linens are so neatly rolled up—some on the ground and others where we placed His head on Friday."

"What does that mean?" asked Magdalene.

"Couldn't be the Roman soldiers," John stated as a matter of fact. "It's too neat. They have no regard for our burial traditions."

Peter began to choke with emotion. "Jesus said that He had to die. And now . . . He's gone, and I abandoned Him." Tears filled his eyes again. "And now we have no idea who stole Him."

"I don't think we'll ever see Him again," said John.

Peter quieted his tears. "That may be true, but we still have to tell the others and then try to find Him."

John nodded. "I wonder how many will believe us?"

"What's to believe?" Peter said. "The body is gone, plain and simple."

"Hurry and tell them," Magdalena said. "I'm too weary to run anymore."

The youngest Apostle could run faster and Peter didn't even try to keep up. He was too old to try. Soon the young man was so far ahead that Peter could barely see him.

"Why are you crying, Peter?" a voice asked.

Terrified, Peter fell to his knees and prostrated himself, saying nothing. He well knew that voice.

After a short wait, Jesus asked, "Aren't you going to speak to me? Are you that afraid?"

"Is it really you, Lord?"

"Yes. Can you see my hands?"

Peter raised his eyes and saw his friend's bloody hands, wide holes straight through. "Yes, my dear Lord, I can see your hands," Peter said, pushing himself onto his knees. "I'm so sorry. For everything. Can you ever forgive me? I am such a foolish and cowardly and prideful man, always speaking and acting before I think."

"You were forgiven long before you even spoke those words."

Peter's hands began to tremble.

"Do not be afraid, Peter. Tell my brothers and sisters to travel to Galilee; there they will all see me on Mt. Tabor."

Without another word, Jesus vanished.

Peter looked in every direction. He was alone on a street and all alone in his knowledge that Jesus had told him that he was for-given. Tears rolled down his face.

Mary Magdalene had remained on her knees outside the en-trance to the tomb for a few moments. Once Peter and John left to tell the others, she slowly stood and peered inside the tomb. There she saw two figures dressed in bright glowing white, sitting where Nicodemus and the others had laid Jesus. One glowing figure knelt where His head had been, the other where His feet had rested.

Was she dreaming? Had she fallen asleep outside the tomb? She shook her head and rubbed her eyes while leaning against the rock wall. The radiant figures were still there.

One of them said, "Why are you weeping?"

"Someone has stolen my Lord," she said. "And I have no idea where they might have taken Him."

She heard the rustle of footsteps behind her and turned to see who it was. She saw that it was a stranger, possibly a gardener.

He said, "Woman, why are you weeping? Who are you looking for?"

Placing her hands over her face she turned back toward the radiant beings, but they had disappeared. She turned back to the stranger.

"I'm looking for my teacher, and for my friend. Sir, if you have taken Him away, please tell me where you left Him, and I will go and remove Him."

"Mary," said the voice.

Now it sounded familiar.

She squinted to focus her eyes on the man who had just spo-ken her name. Her eyes widened and she fell to her knees, tears of joy bursting from her eyes.

"Teacher!" she whispered, throwing herself at His feet and wrapping both arms around His ankles.

"Please do not cling to me," He said. "I have not yet ascended to the Father, to my God and your God."

And then He was gone.

Startled and puzzled by the speed of events, Magdalene continued sobbing as she lay prostrate on the ground. Her mind raced as she thought back over her three different trips to this tomb. Each trip had surprised her, this one most of all.

He had spoken to her. He had risen and He had spoken to her.

And then there were those radiant beings in the tomb. They must have been angels! Why had they been there? Why had they spoken to her? She had no answers. She might never have the answers, but it didn't matter. She had to share what happened here with all those back at the Cenacle. They probably wouldn't believe her, but it was not her place to make them believe. She had born witness to their Redeemer's greatest miracle yet, and she would tell them all.

Perhaps He would appear to others as well. Magdalena knew in her heart that this would not be the only time she would ever see her Teacher again.

As she began her return journey to the Upper Room, she didn't even try to wipe her tears. For the first time since the nightmare that began on Friday, she had hope. Her hope blotted out her grief, her anger, her fear, her despair—even her exhaustion. She hadn't even noticed that she had begun to run as fast as her legs would carry her.

———◆⟆✳⟆◆———

JERUSALEM
UPPER ROOM
EARLY SUNDAY MORNING
33 AD
THE FIRST DAY

When they had awakened this morning, Mary of Zebedee, sisters Martha and Mary, Susanna, and Joanna had found Mary Magdalene gone. Puzzled by her unexplained disappearance, they still had confidence that there had to be a good reason. Magdalena never did anything for herself—always others. They quickly decided that they should carry the burial myrrh, aloes, spices, and linens to Jesus' tomb on their own. They knew it would take a long time because of the awkward weight they had to carry over a route they did not know, but they set off anyway, before the streets began to crowd with foot-traffic.

"Are you sure this is the right way?" Martha asked, struggling with a heavy sack of myrrh.

"We spoke to Joseph of Arimathea just last night," Joanna said. "I'm pretty sure this is the way he told us."

On the road in front of them, a lone figure stood. "Greetings," He said.

All the women dropped what they had been carrying and stood immobile in disbelief. He was dead. Their Jesus had been tortured and crucified and entombed. He was dead. How could He be here? And why? Would He judge them for their absence during His trial and crucifixion?

Weeping confused tears of joy and fear, they ran to their Lord and prostrated themselves on the street, clasping at His feet.

Jesus said, "Do not be afraid. Go and tell all my brothers and sisters to go to Galilee; there they will all see me on Mt. Tabor."

And then they were clasping at nothing, prostrate on an empty street.

He was gone.

The women scrambled to their feet and, abandoning the burial supplies, they raced back to the Upper Room.

When the women arrived and started to announce that Jesus had spoken to them, James couldn't contain himself. "Are you sure it was really Jesus and not the Devil playing a trick on you? Tell me exactly what He said."

"Careful now, my son" Mary of Zebedee said to James. "Remember, everyone in this room is our loving friend, and should be treated accordingly."

"Sorry, ladies," James said, bowing in their direction. "I meant no disrespect."

Joanna decided to answer his question. "Jesus said to us, 'Greetings. Do not be afraid. Go and tell all my brothers and sisters to go to Galilee; there they will all see me on Mt. Tabor.'"

The room turned silent for a few moments.

Finally Simon the Zealot felt the need to speak. "Something doesn't ring true about what you're telling us," he said. "Why would He appear to a group of women—who are not even His Apostles— and give them such a strange message to give to the rest of us? Surely Jesus is fully able to deliver His own messages in person."

Once the Zealot had spoken, John, James, Andrew, and the other Apostles chorused in with similar feelings of their own. They could think of no logical explanation as to why Jesus had only spoken with the women, and concluded that their accounts were probably wishful thinking or grief—maybe even inspired delusions.

Peter said nothing.

The group discussion stopped abruptly when they heard the running footsteps of Mary Magdalene as she dashed up the steps to the Upper Room, shouting between gasps, "I have seen Jesus and He talked with me!"

Everyone ran from the Room to greet Magdalene with hugs and tears of joy at her safe return. Finally, when they had all moved inside to the Upper Room, John couldn't help but say, "Tell us what He said.

Mary Magdalene found a place to sit, still trying to catch her breath, sweat and tears flowing down her face. She told them what had happened once Peter and John left—about the angels who spoke to her while she cried about Jesus being stolen, then the gardener who called her Mary and then turned out to be Jesus who said to her, "Please do not cling to me. I have not yet ascended to the Father, to my God and your God."

And then she shared how He had vanished.

Once again, no one spoke for a few moments.

And now Peter stood from the corner where he had been watching but not speaking. "There it is again," he said. "It seems that our risen Jesus is telling us that He wants to meet with us on Mt. Tabor. It's virtually the same thing He told me after John and I left Magdalene."

"When did you talk with Jesus?" John said.

"While you were running ahead to tell the others about the empty tomb. That's when He appeared and told me that I was forgiven and He wanted to meet with us all on Mt. Tabor."

Each of the disciples had many questions for Magdalene, and soon their tearful and heartfelt exchanges were so noisy that they awakened Mary Clopas who had been napping in a chair beside her sleep-deprived older sister. They needed to be more considerate.

Chapter Twelve

C lopas and his wife Mary lived in Emmaus, some seven miles west of Jerusalem over the rocky hill country. They had come to Jerusalem with many others to joyfully celebrate the Passover festivities. But now that his wife had personally witnessed the crucifixion, entombment, and rigorous preparations for the final burial of Jesus, the longed-for elation from the holiday had long since left her thoughts.

Given the startling events of this morning, Clopas and Mary didn't know what to believe about the news of Jesus rising from death. Most of the male disciples of Jesus had a hard time believing that He had appeared to the women. Clopas and Mary found themselves more than a little bothered by the heated discussions that had taken place earlier that morning. It seemed to them that all His disciples—men and women—should be delighted, inspired, and humbled that Jesus had risen from the dead and had bothered visiting any of them at all. Who He appeared to and when shouldn't make the slightest difference.

Frustrated and disappointed by the bickering of their friends,

Clopas and Mary decided to pack up and return to Emmaus on foot. They bid a loving farewell to all their friends, taking their time with Mother Mary and Mary Magdalene, neither of whom had seemed particularly bothered by the morning's debate. Mother Mary actually looked more at peace than she had all week.

It would take them about half a day to get home, so they expected to arrive sometime around the afternoon meal time. They remained silent for some time after they left Jerusalem.

"Mother Mary seemed her old self when we said goodbye," Clopas said. "She was smiling and gracious. I don't know that I could have done the same had it been my child murdered. And all He ever did was preach love and kindness."

"Mother Mary is very wise," Mary said. "There is nothing else she can do but carry on. Some things are out of our hands. The men of the Sanhedrin and the Temple were scared of Jesus and decided He had to die. There was nothing she could have done to stop them."

"Well, maybe she couldn't have done anything," Clopas said, "but us men could have done something—we were all just too scared. Except John."

"You're right," she said with a smile. "I have no idea what came over him."

Just then a tall stranger dressed like a shepherd walked up beside them and fell in step with the couple.

"Greetings, friends," said the stranger. "What's the news from Jerusalem?"

They stopped walking and Clopas looked at the stranger, frustrated. "Are you the only visitor to the city who does not know what's taken place there in these recent days?"

The stranger seemed surprised. "What sort of things?"

"The things that happened to Jesus the Nazarene. He was a prophet, mighty in deed and word before God and all the people.

Our chief priests and rulers handed Him over to a sentence of death and crucified Him."

"We were hoping He would be the one to redeem Israel," Mary added. "And it is now the third day since all this took place—the day something special was supposed to happen according to Scripture."

Clopas added, "Some women from our group, however, visited His tomb early this morning and did not find His body. They came back and reported that they had indeed seen a vision of the prophet risen, and angels who announced that He was alive."

"But we went to the tomb afterwards. We found things just as the women described, but Him we did not see."

"Oh how foolish you are," said the stranger. "How slow of heart to believe the prophets' words! Was it not necessary that the Messiah should suffer these things to enter into His glory?"

Clopas and Mary studied each other, totally confused by the stranger. He puzzled them—asking all these questions but apparently already highly knowledgeable. He continued walking, head down and said, "Don't you remember when Moses said, 'The Lord your God will raise up for you a prophet like me from among you, from your fellow Israelites, and I will put my words in His mouth. He will tell them everything I command Him?'"

"Yes, of course," Clopas said. "But the rabbis have all taught that this meant God would send someone like King David—someone who would come to liberate us from our oppressors! Yet the Romans still rule over our people with an iron fist!"

The stranger smiled, still gazing at the ground. "You need to open up your minds and hearts. Don't you remember how Daniel spoke of the resurrection? He wrote, 'Multitudes who sleep in the dust of the earth will awake: some to everlasting life.' And what about what King David wrote? 'Because You will not abandon me to the realm of the dead, nor will You let your faithful one see decay.' David also wrote, 'The meek shall eat and be satisfied: they shall praise the Lord. Those that seek Him: your heart shall live forever.'"

The stranger looked up at Clopas and Mary. "Don't you see how the prophets were already talking about resurrection from death *and* life everlasting?"

Mary studied the stranger. "How can life everlasting have any meaning if not on earth? The prophecy speaks of a Redeemer who would deliver us from slavery! And then after our liberation, sincere Israelite believers would be blessed with life on earth that had no end."

"Can't you see how small such an interpretation is?" said the stranger. "That God—maker of all things—would take so much effort just to give Israelites eternal life, on earth, that would be denied anyone who was not Jewish? Is that your vision of God? A God of discrimination and small mindedness?

"You see Him as a God who would build a wall around Israel so that only Jews may enjoy the benefits of everlasting life? Why would the Creator of all the universe do that? Can't you see it would be impossible for an all-loving God to do such a thing?"

Clopas and Mary stared at the stranger.

"I..." Mary stammered. "I hadn't thought of it like that before."

The stranger smiled, then turned to Clopas. "How about you, sir?"

He shrugged. "I don't know what I think. That's the whole problem with this thing about Jesus. I'm just really confused."

The stranger nodded. "Thank you. How refreshing—a man who is willing to admit he doesn't know the answer to a difficult question. That takes real courage."

Clopas smiled. "Maybe it's the start of something good. Tell me more, please. All your references to the Torah and the Scriptures have awakened my mind and heart. I'm afraid I've fallen into bad habits in my faith."

The stranger said, "I'm sorry if I embarrassed you. That was not my intention."

"I know," said Clopas. "The truth is that I've gotten lazy."

The stranger nodded with compassion. "As you wish. Shall we discuss Isaiah, where the prophecy comes from?"

Clopas nodded.

The stranger continued. "Isaiah spoke of how it would be necessary for God to send someone who would both obey and suffer for God. 'Yet it was the Lord's will to crush Him and cause Him to suffer, and though the Lord makes His life an offering for sin, He will see His offspring and prolong His days, and the will of God will prosper in His hand. After He has suffered, He will see the light of life and be satisfied; by His knowledge, my righteous servant will justify many, and He will bear their iniquities.'"

Mary nodded. "Yes, I can see how your interpretation might be what he meant."

The stranger smiled at them. "Good. Now let's look at King David when he wrote: 'Surely your goodness and love will follow me all the days of my life, and I will dwell in the house of the Lord forever.' So where is this house of the Lord?"

Clopas took a deep breath. "In Heaven, I suppose. That's the only place it could be."

"Exactly," said the stranger, "Moses says the same thing in Psalm 91 where he begins: 'You who dwell in the shelter of the Most High, who abide in the shadow of the Almighty,' and ends, 'With length of days I will satisfy them and show them my saving power.' He's saying that those 'in the shelter of the Most High,' will live there forever."

Mary smiled. "So their intent was to prepare us for a Messiah—not of this world—who had a message for us about Heaven and how we can get there. Am I on the right path?"

The stranger smiled. "You're making good progress, but I think we should stop and find some shade and drink a little water. This sun is blazing. Maybe after we've cooled off a bit and put some fresh water in our sweaty bodies, things might become a little clearer."

"I like that idea," said Clopas.

And so they located some shade just off the road and rested for a short while. Fortunately, Clopas and Mary had packed plenty of water and offered some to the stranger.

"Thank you, but I'm not thirsty."

"We have plenty," Mary said.

"I'm fine. Please accept my sincere thanks."

"We should be going," Clopas said after a short time. Turning to the tall man, he said, "But we don't want our talk to end. You've opened our minds and hearts and now we're beginning to see things in a different light. You don't mind explaining more about the Scriptures to us, do you?"

"Not at all," said the stranger in shepherd's clothing. "Let's go back to Moses and work our way toward the present. Would that be helpful for you?"

Mary and Clopas smiled.

"We certainly appreciate your spending so much time patiently explaining things," Mary said.

And so, the stranger began again. Beginning with Moses and the prophets, He outlined the many places in Scriptures that alluded to the promised savior and the fact that such a Messiah would have to die in order to open eternal life to all peoples. The time and distance passed quickly.

As they approached Emmaus, the stranger indicated that his ultimate destination lay further west. This caused Clopas and Mary great concern.

"It's late in the day," Clopas said. "We would be most pleased if you would spend the night and allow us to give you a meal in our home."

"After all the time you've spent explaining so much," Mary said, "we would consider it a great honor if you would accept our thankful hospitality."

The stranger smiled. "Well, alright. I'm happy and delighted to accept your gracious invitation, but I must be on my way early in the morning."

When they finally arrived at the Clopas home and washed their feet, Clopas poured wine for everyone while Mary quickly organized a supper of lentils, honey, cheese, dried fish, and some bread she had baked and stored before they had departed for Jerusalem. When she had set out the food, they all sat down at the table and gave thanks to God for the food and their safe return home. The stranger then took the bread, broke it, and gave it to Clopas and Mary saying, "Take and eat: this is my body."

With that, they stared at the stranger. How could they not have seen it? This was Jesus! Terrified and speechless, they fell to their knees and prostrated themselves.

Silence was the only response.

Looking up, they quickly realized they were now alone. Jesus had vanished.

Still speechless and overwhelmed, they turned to each other and hugged. Tears began to roll down Mary's face and she said, "Were not our hearts burning within us? The whole time it was Him!"

"He opened the Scriptures to us," Clopas murmured.

"He did," said Mary. She looked her husband in the eyes, resolute. "We must leave at once! We have to return to Jerusalem to tell the others! This changes everything!"

JERUSALEM
THE CENACLE
JUST AFTER THE EVENING MEAL
33 AD
THE FIRST DAY

Clopas and Mary borrowed two donkeys and rushed back to the Upper Room, where they found many disciples, including the Apostles, still in heated discussions behind locked doors.

As the couple from Emmaus entered the room, Mary Magdalene addressed them. "I thought you left to return to your home this morning?"

"We did," said Mary Clopas, "but then something incredible happened."

And after the Clopas couple revealed their experience with their Redeemer on the road, the room fell silent.

As though He had been there in the room the whole time, Jesus stepped forward from the corner of the room and stood among them, for all to see.

"Peace be with you," He said.

Many of the men and women fell to their knees, crying with delight, but others gasped in fear, and muttered that they were seeing a ghost.

"Why are you troubled?" He said, loud enough for all to hear. "And why do questions arise in your hearts? Look at my hands and feet." He exposed His limbs for all to see. "Can you not see that it is I, myself? Touch me and see. A ghost does not have flesh and bones as you can see I have."

Most now cowered in corners of the room, afraid of what their senses told them, despite wanting to be overjoyed—wanting this to really be their friend and teacher.

"Have you anything to eat?" He asked.

Mary Magdalene ran and brought Him a piece of baked fish, which He took and ate.

Silence filled the room again as He finished His food.

Then He said to them, "These are my words that I spoke to you while I was still with you, that everything written about me in the Law of Moses and in the prophets and psalms must be fulfilled." Then He spoke to them for some time, reiterating much about the Scriptures that He had imparted on Clopas and Mary. And He concluded by saying, "Thus it is written that the Messiah would suffer and rise from the dead on the third day. And that repentance, and the forgiveness of sins, would be preached in His name to all the nations, beginning in Jerusalem. You are witnesses to these things. And behold I am sending the promise of my Father upon you."

Jesus then looked around the room, puzzlement on His face.

"What's the matter?" asked Mary Magdalene.

"I see that Thomas is missing. I would like to speak with him."

No sooner had He spoken, then He vanished.

CHAPTER THIRTEEN

JERUSALEM
UPPER ROOM
33 AD
THE SECOND DAY

The next time Thomas decided to return to the Upper Room, he knocked quietly on the locked front door. He knew their fear of the soldiers—he was afraid too. He had been looking over his shoulder for the past several days and had barely slept. By continuing to associate with Jesus' movement, Thomas was putting his entire family in jeopardy. He wasn't sure he could continue. What was the point anymore? What's a movement without its leader?

He knocked again, a little louder this time.

"Don't worry," he whispered through the door. "It's only me—Thomas."

The door opened and John let him in, rushing him inside and quickly locking it again.

Peter greeted him with a big bear hug. "We've all missed you. Are you well?"

"I'm fine," he said. "I've come in the hope that everyone feels a little more friendly today. All that arguing yesterday between brothers and sisters who are supposed to be followers of Jesus made me uncomfortable."

"That's too bad," said Magdalene. "Jesus came here last night and asked about you."

Thomas squinted at her, then looked around the room. No one was laughing. "I find that hard to believe," he said. "Why would Jesus want to talk to me?"

Mother Mary crossed the room to him and embraced him. "Magdalena speaks the truth. My Son did appear last night. He asked why you were absent... We all need to be together right now. When one of us is missing, all of us feel incomplete."

"I'm sorry, Mother," Thomas said. "I had no intention of offending anyone, least of all our dearly departed friend and Teacher, but I was not the only absence yesterday. There was also an absence of trust, and of kindness, with regard to who Jesus appeared to and who did or didn't see Him. It sounded to me like He appeared to several people He trusted and then when others discovered they were not included among those He appeared to, they reacted with accusations and jealousy. Have we all collectively agreed who we believe now?"

"We believe them all," James said. "You're right. Emotions did run high. We're all scared for our lives right now. But the truth is there's not a single person here who would look any of the rest of us in the eye and tell us something that wasn't true."

"Happy to hear it," said Thomas, hiding his discomfort. He had hoped to use their in-fighting as an excuse to leave. He looked around the room and took a deep breath. "Now may I say something true that needs to be heard?"

The others nodded, somber faces rapt with attention. He couldn't do it. He couldn't just announce he was leaving. Not now. He looked around the room and seized upon the first thought that sprung to mind.

"Mary Magdalene," Thomas continued, focusing his attention to her, "when I last saw you, you were sorely in need of sleep. Has that been remedied?"

Magdalene laughed along with the rest of the room and nodded. "Yes, Thomas. You're right, it wasn't good for me, staying awake three nights in a row. It all began to blur together, became one long horrible day. I'd begun to fear I was trapped in a nightmare by the end, unsure of what further horrors might await me if I dared to lay my head down and close my eyes. But I slept soundly last night. Peacefully, even. But only because Jesus came to us last night—through locked doors—and all of us saw Him."

"What do you mean 'through locked doors'?" Thomas said.

Clopas walked up to Thomas, draped an arm over his shoulders, and said, "Last night we all assembled here in this room with the doors and windows locked, talking and discussing what we had seen—He appeared to my wife and I on the road to our home—and then, suddenly, there was Jesus. Standing in the middle of the room. Talking to us."

Thomas scowled. "Just like that?"

"Not only did my Son simply appear," said Mother Mary, "but He invited us to inspect His hands and feet—to see His wounds. He even ate some fish! Just to prove He wasn't a ghost!"

"Well *we* weren't worried about whether or not He was a ghost," said Mary Clopas. "My husband and I had already had a meal with Him yesterday afternoon in Emmaus."

"It was our Jesus, risen," said Peter. "The same un-bloodied Jesus we'd all been walking with these years. Yes, He had wounds on His hands and feet, but He walked painlessly around the room, dressed in His usual head wrap, tunic, and sandals... It was Him, Thomas."

Thomas scratched his head and began to pace. "I hear what you're saying, but I don't believe it."

"Thomas, I swear to you," said Peter, "it was Him! Where is your faith?"

Thomas turned and stared daggers at him. "Don't you dare talk to me of faith. You had your hour of weakness, Peter, and you were forgiven. I hope you will forgive mine now. Unless I see the nail marks on His hands and put my finger where the nails were, and put my hand into His side, I cannot believe you."

"Well," said John, "I guess you will need to stay here until Jesus returns. Don't forget, He told us He wants to talk with you."

Thomas shrugged. "Well, here I am."

JERUSALEM
UPPER ROOM
33 AD
THE EIGHTH DAY

A week had passed since Jesus' last visit, and once again the disciples had assembled for an evening meal behind locked doors and windows. When they weren't sharing a meal, most of them spent their time praying for guidance or discussing the best way forward for their movement.

But many of them, like Thomas, had trouble accepting the fact that Jesus had risen from the tomb and now presented Himself seemingly at random throughout Jerusalem and its surrounding areas. None of what Jesus did and said made sense to these confused disciples. The risen Jesus was not at all what they expected from their Messiah. Clopas and his wife explained what Jesus had taught them on the road as best they could, but their Teacher had spoken with such eloquence and knowledge of Scripture, they had no way of replicating what He said.

On the more practical side, none of them could ignore the fact that Roman soldiers and agents of the Sanhedrin continued to stalk them night and day, itching to catch any of them isolated and away from the crowds of the city. They had confirmed through Susanna and Joanna's connections that the Jewish leaders had bribed the Roman guard detail at the tomb. Some of the Jewish leaders were furious that Joseph of Arimathea had escaped and hoped to catch him returning to his family's crypt, but had not acted further to recapture the holy man. What seemed to keep them at bay was the serious possibility of a major uprising. Word of Jesus' rising had spread, one whisper at a time, throughout the streets of Jerusalem. This posed a significant threat to the safety of all followers of Jesus, but especially of Lazarus.

Lazarus had heard rumors that Caiaphas and his family wanted to kill him because he was the one person who could speak with absolute authority to the power of Jesus to raise to life those who died. According to Joanna and Susanna, anyone caught in the company of Lazarus or who might have the gall to hide him in their home could expect deadly consequences.

Nonetheless, Lazarus remained welcome and protected at the Cenacle. The other disciples believed Jesus must have raised Lazarus from death for a reason—other than a demonstration of His power. Jesus did not indulge such vanities. Lazarus was grateful for the disciples' sanctuary and protection, but he was not sure what to think. All he knew was that he had died, and Jesus the Nazarene had pulled him from the peace of death.

Born the youngest sibling of his family, Lazarus of Bethany was in his mid-twenties. He'd never quite recovered from the loss of both parents to disease during his teenage years. Depression settled in and his internal struggle to cope became the predominant impression he left with most he encountered. He was not delighted to have been brought back to life by Jesus. What he experienced as he lay dead in his tomb had been relief. He had let go of everything—his grief, his loneliness, his feeling of never quite belonging, his responsibilities—he had been cleansed of it all. When he had been forced back into his body, he found only new loneliness waiting for him, along with new responsibilities. And now he would certainly never belong.

But it made his sisters very happy to have him back and alive, so as usual he kept his feelings to himself. He loved them beyond all else—his brief experience of happiness in death would have to await God's will. His sisters were determined to keep him safe from further harm, so he once again adopted solitude as an approach to life.

But when Peter, Andrew, and James of Zebedee showed up at the family home, hiding from the men of the Sanhedrin, everything changed. Now that they too were targets, these were men with whom he could truly identify. Yes, he'd met them all before when Jesus and his followers showed up at the family home to share a meal or a special occasion, but he'd never had the chance to actually get to know them. He had relished sharing his expertise at hiding, one of the few things he was good at. The three Apostles were grateful at the time, of course, but he did not realize how upsetting his presence was for many of them.

Thomas sat across the room from Lazarus, staring at him—scowling. Lazarus said nothing. Tensions had begun to grow again. Jesus had appeared and promised to return, but a week had passed and He had yet to make good on His promise.

Thomas sighed and stood up from his chair. "I can't believe I let you all convince me to stay this long," he muttered, rubbing his hands over his face. "I can't believe I've been risking my family for this."

Someone stepped forward, into Thomas' path. It was Jesus.

"Peace be with you," He said, looking around the room. "Hello Thomas. I am glad to finally be able to speak with you. Come here, please." He motioned for Thomas to come to His side. "Put your finger here; see my hands. Reach out your hand and put it into my side. Stop doubting and believe."

Tears welled up in Thomas' eyes. He fell to his knees, gazing up at Jesus. "My Lord and my God!"

Jesus smiled, a little sadly, it seemed to Lazarus. "Because you have seen me, you have believed. Blessed are those who have not seen and yet have believed."

An uneasy silence filled the room.

Jesus then turned to the rest of the room and said to them, "These are my words that I spoke to you while I was still with you: everything written about me in the Law of Moses and in the prophets and psalms must be fulfilled."

Next He opened their minds to understand Scripture, repeating much of what Clopas and his wife had been trying to communicate over the past week, and finally He said to them, "Thus it is written that the Messiah would suffer and rise from the dead on the third day. And that repentance, and the forgiveness of sins, would be preached in His name to all the nations, beginning in Jerusalem. You are witnesses to these things. And behold I am sending the promise of my Father upon you.

"Go to Galilee; there you will see me again." And just as quickly as He came, Jesus vanished.

JERUSALEM
THE RESIDENCE OF JOANNA
MID-AFTERNOON
33 AD
THE ELEVENTH DAY

Joanna and Susanna knew that remaining silent about the problem of Lazarus could not continue, so they invited Mary and

Martha of Bethany, Magdalena, and Procula to Joanna's home. No one would disturb them there.

Once the wine had been poured and finger foods served, Joanna asked a servant to close all doors.

Joanna began, "Thank you, ladies, for coming on such short notice. As followers of Jesus, each of us knows that any problem within the movement that poses the potential for loss of life for any of us is a problem for all. Such a problem has arisen and we must discuss it before it's too late: Lazarus is what I'm talking about."

She studied Martha and Mary of Bethany, who appeared nervous and in need of sleep.

"I'm sorry," Joanna said, still looking directly at them, "but you have to know your brother's life is in serious jeopardy. As is the life of anyone around him. It's not your fault. There's nothing you could have done differently to change that. The fact is that Caiaphas and his father-in-law are evil men and will stop at nothing to attain their goals—no matter how insane or illegal. They have murdered our Redeemer, but there are still loose ends they are hungry to tie up. Your brother is one such loose end."

Martha and Mary began to cry.

"That's why we're having this meeting!" Susanna interjected, trying to calm the sisters. "To find a way to save his life!"

The two sisters wiped their eyes.

"You're certain he's still in danger?" Martha asked.

"He would not need to hide if he were not," said Susanna.

"Procula," said Joanna. "Please, tell us what you know."

Procula took a deep breath. "Well, each of you knows that anything said here stays here. Right?"

Everyone nodded their agreement.

Procula continued. "I have reliable information that Caiaphas and Annas have once again hired the Pagan soldiers they used to arrest Joseph of Arimathea—only this time, they've hired them to assassinate Lazarus and anyone else who happens to be in his company."

"When did all that happen with Joseph?" Magdalena asked, astonishment written across her face. "One of the nicest men I've ever met."

"About a week ago," said Procula.

"I thought you knew," said Susanna.

"I thought everybody knew," said Joanna. "I heard Lazarus talking about it with Peter just last night."

"Where is Joseph now?" Martha said.

"Getting as far away from this city as possible," said Susanna.

Magdalena frowned. "Didn't you just say Joseph was arrested?"

Susanna and Procula nodded. Joanna smirked. "He had help and is no longer imprisoned," she said matter-of-factly. "And let's just let it go at that."

"Goodness," said Mary of Bethany. "I can see there's been a lot going on this past week that I know nothing about."

"Sorry," said Susanna. "I honestly thought you all knew."

"Not at all," said Mary of Bethany. "Honestly, I think I'd rather not know. Back to our brother: does anyone have an idea of how we can keep him safe? Truly safe?"

The room went silent for a few moments.

"I have an idea," said Mary Magdalene.

"Please," said Martha, "we've run out of ideas other than keeping him at the Cenacle."

"I'd rather not speak of details," Magdalena replied. "But he needs to get out of town."

"What do you mean?" said Martha. "Where would he go?"

"The less you know, the safer your brother will be," Magdala said.

"She's right," said Procula. "I know these men. All such men are the same—their lust for power, for control, eclipses their conscience—especially when there's big money involved, which, I assure you, is the case. If they were to catch you, they would torture the information out of you. And the law would be on their side."

The two sisters looked horrified.

"So here's my proposal," Magdalena said, looking directly at Martha and Mary. "You explain to Lazarus that mercenaries have been hired to kill him. As long as he's in Jerusalem, it could happen any second—even as we speak. Tell him you've made arrangements for him to escape, provided he's willing to entrust himself to me. He must come with me and do *exactly* as I tell him. If he does, I can guarantee his safety."

"What if he doesn't follow your instructions?" Martha said.

"Then...we'll both probably die," Magdala said, raising her eyebrows.

Once again, the room went silent.

"Are we ever going to see him again?" Mary asked.

Magdalena sighed and avoided their eyes. "As long as Caiaphas and his family remain in power, it's unlikely you'll see him again."

Tears welled up in the sisters' eyes.

"Bear in mind," Magdalena added, "the future of Lazarus is about life and death. Jesus came on this earth to die on the cross to give us the keys to our Father's Kingdom in Heaven. Kindness, love, forgiveness—those are the keys to life everlasting. Everything He does is about kindness, love, and forgiveness—including returning your brother to life. Whatever He has planned for Lazarus will not come to pass unless your brother remains alive. And God's plan for him cannot happen in Jerusalem. If he remains, sooner or later these hired killers will find him. As surely as the sun will rise in the morning, they will find him."

Mary and Martha wept quietly, but were nodding.

"I realize that this is terrible news for you both," Magdalena said. "And I apologize if my words seem harsh, but I am convinced he will be murdered, soon, unless we do something drastic. Today. Something men like Caiaphas would never expect. But if you think my suggestion is bad or wrong, I'm more than willing to stand aside."

Martha and Mary sniffed and wiped their eyes. "You're willing to risk your life to save our brother," Mary of Bethany sobbed. "That's... I can't even begin to find the right words."

Martha cleared her throat and spoke softly. "I don't hear anyone else here with another suggestion. I know my sister and I don't have one. And we've been racking our brains night and day ever since Jesus decided to vacate the Arimathea family crypt."

Mary of Bethany wiped her eyes and put an arm around her sister. "God brought us here tonight for a reason, dear sister—it's time to let our brother go. We've been praying for him since Jesus brought him back to life. And it seems, dearest Mary of Magdala, that you're the answer to our prayers. Thank you. Thank you so very much."

Magdalena shook her head, her face hot with emotions. "I'm no gift. Jesus is the gift. He blessed me with experiences and people in my life who have helped me—far beyond what I had any reason to expect. Far beyond what I thought I deserved. He saved me. I'm just trying to give back because... because it's what He would have done."

Procula wiped her eyes and said, "This needs to happen today."

"Procula's right," Joanna said. "Martha and Mary, you should stay here. From this moment on, we must assume these assassins are lying in wait around every corner of the city. As Lazarus' sisters, roaming the streets isn't safe for you. Magdalena, the logistical and out-of-pocket costs of this plan will be borne by Susanna and myself. Whatever you need."

Magdalena nodded. "Thank you."

"Please prepare a complete list of everything you're going to need," Joanna continued. "We will need it before you leave this house. And don't be bashful about what you ask for—money is no object. Like we said before, we're all in this together. Each of us will be making a huge sacrifice."

Next, Joanna turned to Martha and Mary, tears still in their eyes. "Keep in mind we cannot delay. This is happening now. Talk to Magdalena and work out the details of how and when you're going to introduce Lazarus to his new guardian. We realize how hard this will be, but this really is life and death."

Susanna cleared her throat and turned to Procula. "Let's not forget the huge chance the governor's wife took by being here today. Her assessment of the city's elites and her passing of highly sensitive information have been invaluable, but under no circumstances can she be found out. Everyone in the movement—not just the leaders—would be crucified." And raising her voice for emphasis, Susanna said, "So, let us all mind our tongues and body language. The slightest mistake will doom us all."

"And on that note," Joanna said, "before our work truly begins, let us all kneel in prayer. For the safe execution of Magdalena's plan, and for protection. God, please watch over us all."

And they did.

Chapter Fourteen

The number of disciples staying at the Cenacle had already begun to diminish, which worried those who remained. Already missing were Martha, Mary, and Lazarus of Bethany, Mary Magdalene, Clopas and his wife, and nobody had seen Longinus in days.

The conversations dragged on endlessly, often interrupted by long pauses while many of those present considered and weighed what another had just said. Each felt certain the risen Jesus would appear again soon because He had told them to go to Galilee where they would see Him—and possibly have a chance to ask Him questions—they hoped.

Most had seen Jesus, but the question remained: had they really seen and talked with the Jesus they'd known before His crucifixion? And furthermore, where was the Messiah Savior they and their forefathers had been promised going back centuries? Jesus had told them about a kingdom not of this world, but what about this world? The place in which each of them and their families had to live daily in fear and oppression?

Peter had joined the ranks of the doubters, as had James of Zebedee, Nathaniel, Phillip, Matthew, Simon the Zealot, and Thaddeus. Mother Mary did her best to keep all conversations civil and kind, but the constant acrimony was beginning to visibly take its toll on her.

Finally, John spoke up, "I think we should take a break, get some sleep, and resume this discussion in the morning while we prepare for our trip to Galilee."

Mother Mary nodded and looked around the room. "I think that's a good idea, John. I know I could certainly use some more sleep."

Peter took a deep breath. "I agree."

Just as he stood to retire for the night, there was a knock at the front door. Everyone scurried to their various emergency hiding places.

"Who is it?" said John, walking to the door.

"It's us, Joanna and Susanna. Can we come in?"

John unbolted the door. "Of course you can come in," he said with a wide grin. "Where have you been?"

"Taking care of some personal business," Susanna said. Once they were safely inside, John bolted the door behind them. "We think we may have been followed, but we ran down a few narrow streets we chose at random and hid for well over an hour. If there was anyone there, I'm pretty sure they moved on."

Joanna took a deep breath and walked over to Mother Mary. "Is it true that you asked Joseph of Arimathea to try and find anything he could from Golgotha that belonged to Jesus?"

Mother Mary raised her eyebrows and looked apprehensive. "Yes, I did—days ago. I'd forgotten all about it. Why do you ask?"

"Well, in typical Joseph fashion, *he* didn't forget. His family sent me this earlier today—they had it washed before giving it to us."

From a leather carrying pouch, Joanna pulled out a scarlet tunic.

Mother Mary's eyes went wide and her face glowed. She grabbed the garment from Joanna's hands and clutched it to her heart. "Oh my dear Jesus," she whispered. "I gifted this to Him, just before He rode into Jerusalem on that donkey! Seems like an eternity ago..." She looked up at Joanna and Susanna. "Thank you so very much, both of you. I can't thank you enough. And Joseph too—dear man."

She turned and walked toward her bedroom, weeping, but midway there, wobbled and collapsed to the floor. Joanna, Susanna, and John all rushed to her side, lifting her up off the wooden floor. Together, they carried Mother Mary to her room, while others ran to fetch water and smelling salts. In a matter of minutes she was wide awake again.

"Sorry about that everyone," she said, blushing with embarrassment. She took a long drink of water. "I guess I was a lot more tired than I thought." She giggled self-consciously.

"Get some rest, Mother," John said, taking her water from her shaky hands.

Mother Mary smiled, still clutching the tunic to her chest. "Thank you, dear John. You're always worrying about me. But the time has come. My Son wants to meet with you and the others. You need to go. To Galilee."

"Don't worry about being left alone," said Susanna. "Joanna and I will make sure there's always someone here with you. We love you."

Mother Mary smiled. "Thank you. I love you too." She looked around again. "Is Mary Magdalene here? I haven't seen her lately."

"She's fine," said Joanna. "She came to my house just the other day."

Mother Mary nodded at the news. "I'm glad to hear she's

alright." She closed her eyes and pulled up the covers. "She certainly keeps herelf busy."

※

JERUSALEM
THE EMPTY JESUS TOMB
MID-EVENING
33 AD
THE THIRTEENTH DAY

Mary Magdalene had thought things through—as she always did—and concluded that she had several things going for her.

First of all, Caiaphas and his family had no idea what Lazarus actually looked like. Magdalena had nearly doubled over in laughter when Procula had divulged this tidbit to her. Fortunately for her plan, Lazarus had no distinguishing physical features—nor did he have any well-known bad habits. So even if someone gave a decent description of him, it would fit thousands of other young men in their mid-twenties who lived and worked around Jerusalem.

Secondly, she had the element of surprise on her side. Oh sure, rumors had circulated that Caiaphas and his family strongly disliked Lazarus and his witness about Jesus bringing him back to life. But Caiaphas and Annas had no idea anyone other than themselves knew of their true commitment to actually murder Lazarus.

Thirdly, thanks to Susanna, Joanna, and Procula, Magdalena knew the arrogance of how these men thought. After all, they'd caught Jesus and His followers off guard, and they'd caught Joseph of Arimathea and his family off guard. Why? Because Caiaphas and his crowd always went to such great lengths to remind everyone in the city that they were Holy Men of God. Their rank and status were their mask and alibi.

Fourthly, she had prayed. Harder than she had ever prayed in her life.

But just to make sure she hadn't overlooked any detail, Magdalena picked a place to meet with Lazarus and his sisters that no one would think of. Somewhere off the beaten path so the sisters would have a chance to bid their brother a proper good-bye.

The sisters had agreed that they would bring Lazarus and say their goodbyes at nine in the evening at the now abandoned Arimathea family tomb Jesus had once occupied. She was waiting in the dark when the two women arrived with their brother holding a burning torch. They also brought a large male servant for protection.

"Kill that torch!" Magdalena hissed at them. "No one can know we're meeting here—not even by accident."

Lazarus did as she asked.

"Thank you," Magdala said. "Have you brought everything on my list?"

Lazarus and his sisters nodded.

Magdala watched Lazarus for a moment. "Your sisters have gone over the ground rules for this journey?"

Lazarus nodded.

"So as to avoid any possible misunderstanding: Lazarus, you understand how disciplined we're going to have to be in order to pull this off and not be killed?"

Again Lazarus nodded.

"That means whatever order I give you, you follow it immediately and to the letter—no questions asked. Are we clear?"

Lazarus studied Magdalena for a moment. "Absolutely clear," he said. "I put myself in your hands."

Magdala took a deep breath. "Okay then. This is it. I'll give you some privacy. Please keep your farewells brief. We're on a tight schedule and need to get going."

She walked away from the siblings toward grove of trees that would be out of earshot. She did not envy the siblings their current heartbreak—to have one's brother die, then returned to life, only to have to say goodbye forever soon thereafter.

But this was more important than their sorrow.

In a way, Lazarus was Jesus' legacy embodied. And Magdalena would do everything in her power to protect that.

After a few minutes, Martha called out, barely loud enough to be heard, "Okay, we're ready."

Magdalena walked back to where they were standing. "Okay ladies. When you leave, make sure no one sees you. Do not re-light that torch until you're far enough from here that we cannot see it. In fact, if you can help it, don't re-light it at all. The moon is beginning to shine through the clouds, so it may not be necessary."

She gave Martha and Mary a big hug. "You were never here. You have not seen me in days and have no idea where your brother is. Joanna and Susanna have volunteered to let you continue to stay with them until it's safe. Only when I've had a chance to send word should you even consider returning home. Until then, you need to attend all meetings with the rest of the disciples and carry on your personal lives as if nothing were different."

She studied their tear-streaked faces. "The success of this plan depends entirely on you both. You cannot let on to anyone—including your servants." Nodding at the large male servant who had accompanied them. "Present company excepted, but make sure he has extra incentive to remain mute."

The sisters nodded.

"Okay then," Magdalena said. "It's time for you to depart. I'll send word as soon as it's safe. Please keep us in your constant prayers."

The sisters nodded and, with a final look at their brother, departed with their large servant.

It was pitch dark when the moon went behind the clouds, and so quiet it felt as though there was no one else in the world besides Lazarus and herself.

"Now what?" Lazarus said finally.

She looked around nervously, then let out a brief, shrill whistle.

Out of a dark cluster of trees came Longinus, leading three horses. The centurion wore head-to-toe gladiator battle gear, and one of the horses he led was the big, black Arabian he had ridden atop Golgotha. His horse was fitted with leather battle gear on the neck, front, and rear quarters to protect the animal should they run into trouble. Longinus himself carried a sword and spear.

"Awaiting your command, my lady," said the centurion.

JUDEA
THE ROAD TO GALILEE
DUSK
33 AD
THE FIFTEENTH DAY

The Apostles knew only too well the walk from Jerusalem to Galilee would take the better part of a week. They had walked that distance, and others like it, with Jesus many times these past years. As was their normal routine when making such treks, they broke into the usual grouping: Peter, James, Andrew, and John; Phillip, Bartholomew, Matthew, and Thomas; and lastly, James of Alphaeus, Jude, and Simon the Zealot. Judas would have walked with this last group.

Peter thought of Judas often. He'd contemplated suicide himself—but he'd been blessed by the gift of forgiveness from Jesus—despite his unworthiness.

Judas' fate weighed heavy on Peter's mind and he found himself occasionally falling behind his group, as they tended to walk faster than the others. Most of them scuffled along the road toward their destination in silence, offering an occasional thought to the others of their groups. Peter imagined their heads were swarming with heavy thoughts of their own. After all, their world had just been turned upside down.

As Judeans, they had all been indoctrinated since childhood with the idea that their savior was going to be a militaristic Messiah—a conqueror and liberator, like King David. As a subjugated people, the Jews were born into a life of exhaustion and anger—in constant fear for their lives and their loved ones.

Instead, they got a Messiah whose only weapons were kindness, love, and forgiveness.

Forgiveness.

If Peter was honest, he was still having trouble accepting the forgiveness Jesus conferred on him. Peter had been so certain he would never abandon his dearest friend. And yet there could be no doubt that he had done just that. How could Jesus possibly forgive him? That wasn't justice! It wasn't right! He should've been hanged right next to Judas!

But he'd run through this same string of thoughts before. Over and over.

He swallowed a lump in his throat and tried not to think about the missing Judas and his pain.

Jesus taught radical and unconditional love. And here it was, in action: forgiveness.

Peter looked up from his thoughts and saw they were passing Jericho and heading north, alongside the Jordan.

Looking over to John, he called out to him and jogged over to walk beside him. "Can I ask you something?" Peter said. "What happened inside you that made you stay with Jesus that night?"

The young man shrugged. "I don't know. It just seemed like the right thing to do. He was all alone. Someone had to stay with Him, and I was already there—I went and told the women first, though."

"Weren't you scared?" Peter asked.

John slowly shook his head side-to-side. "Scared? I have no idea. I just couldn't leave Him alone—that's the only thing that kept going through my mind."

"But how could you not be scared?" Peter said. "Those men could have sent their soldiers to kill you at any moment!"

"Not really," said Andrew, who was walking nearby with James. "Looking back, I should have realized: Caiaphas and his friends couldn't do things according to Mosaic Law because of Passover. The people would have rioted. So they moved quickly, outside the Law, before large numbers of us could seriously challenge them. They pushed for crucifixion because crucifixions take until mid-afternoon, late enough that without proper burial preparations in place, He would be thrown into a mass grave the same day and become a forgotten man."

"Nicodemus and Joseph of Arimathea spoke up for Jesus," John said. "And took care of His body. But that night, we remained a small few against the many acting outside the Law."

"I'll give you one thing, John," said James. "You are a man of the moment, doing what needs to be done right then. The rest of us are too busy thinking, so we do nothing, and become fools."

"You're not fools," said John. "Fear freezes everyone. Look how many times I've made a mess of things when we're fishing because I'm afraid I'm going to make a mistake, and then I do!"

James put his huge, muscular arm around John's shoulder. "But you learn fast, little brother, and that's all anyone can ask."

"I think I now understand why you didn't run away with the rest of us," said Peter, with a quiet laugh. "Because you are the living embodiment of what Jesus meant in His parable of the talents—a 'good and faithful servant.'"

John stared at Peter and smiled bashfully.

Andrew smiled. "Well said, Peter. I think you've hit on something important."

"Speaking of you and fishing," Peter said to John. "I miss it. Life was so much simpler when all we had to concern ourselves with were boats, nets, the winds, and the tide." Peter looked at the sun, racing down the edge of the sky toward the horizon. "We're a bit ahead of schedule. Anyone care to go fishing with me? I think it could help relax us and relieve some tension—doing something we know."

"I need time to rest," said James. "It's been a long trip since we left Jerusalem. I could also use some quiet time to think on everything that's happened since they killed our Jesus."

"Didn't you just say we all think too much and act too little?" Peter countered. "Come on, go fishing with me!"

"We still haven't reached agreement," said Andrew, "on what really happened since they buried Him."

"What's to agree on?" said Peter. "He came back! We made this trip to come see Him because He came back and told us to meet Him here!"

"So you believe now?" John asked.

"I'm here, aren't I?"

Andrew eyed Peter, then turned to face John and the others. "I think some time to ponder and talk and pray about what we've all seen and heard would bring us all great benefit."

The others nodded in accord.

Peter huffed and looked out at the water of the Jordan, thinking of simpler times. He did not want to ponder the last week and a half anymore.

Chapter Fifteen

Jerusalem
The Empty Jesus Tomb
Shortly Before Midnight
33 AD
The Fourteenth Day

ary Magdalene smirked to herself when she saw the shocked look on Lazarus' face.

"So here's the plan," she began. "By the way, can you ride?"

Longinus approached, leading three horses, his big black and two smaller coursers, a chestnut and a gray. Each had obviously been trained for experienced riders, possibly even for battle.

Lazarus nodded. "We've had horses since before our parents died."

"Good," said Magdalena. "I hoped as much, but didn't want to ask anyone for obvious reasons." She studied the young man and his wide-eyed expression. "I'm glad to see that you wore boots. We're both going to need them."

"My sisters made me," he said. "They didn't say anything about horses."

"Your sisters didn't know about the horses," she said. "I've made arrangements for us to ride to Joppa and put you on a ship for Cyprus early tomorrow. From there, you'll be offered free passage to anywhere in Europe, your choice. At no time in this journey will you be left to fend for yourself or allowed to be unattended by friends—all of whom are responsible adults. I want you to feel at ease—as much as possible—and that you're safe."

She stopped talking, taking in Lazarus' scowl. "What's the matter? Am I going too fast in how I'm presenting this?"

"No... It's just... Well, who is this man?" He pointed to Longinus. "What's his role in all this?"

"I'm sorry. This is Longinus." Magdalena stood aside so the two males could shake hands. "He used to be a Roman soldier, but has decided to use his considerable skills to assist those of us who were friends of Jesus—just like your sisters. Longinus is one of us and will be our bodyguard and guide between here and Joppa. He will then accompany me on my way back to Jerusalem."

"I see," Lazarus said, processing all this information. He was especially taken by the impressive physical presence of Longinus and his vast array of battle tools.

"He doesn't speak a lot," Magdalena said. "Mostly he just listens and pays attention to what's going on around him and those he's responsible for. You have any questions you want to ask him?"

Lazarus shrugged. "No, not now."

"Good. As a trained and experienced soldier, he will be the final authority for everything we do—no matter what. If he tells us to do something, it is for our safety and we will do it immediately, no questions asked. Understood?"

He appeared a little dazed but nodded.

"Good. We haven't a second to waste and I would really like to leave and get as far away from the band of murderers hunting you as soon as possible."

"Let's go," Longinus said in his deep baritone voice, indicating they should mount their horses. "Until I say otherwise, we proceed in single file. Mary, you're behind me, Lazarus next. We need to keep a horse length separation for now, so you can hear what I say." He paused and looked to make sure both Mary and Lazarus had properly mounted—boots in stirrups, reins correctly in hand.

"For now, we're just going to walk the horses so as to minimize the noise. Do not fall behind. We ride in silence. I'm the only one who should speak, unless there's an emergency. God willing, that won't happen."

With that, they walked their horses from the garden along the city's north wall and out onto the northwestern road to Joppa. The only sounds they made were the clopping of hoofs onto the hard, dry earth. There had been no rain for weeks. Their only light was the moon, flickering slowly as clouds swept across the night sky.

After about half an hour, Longinus held up his hand, signaling Mary and Lazarus to bring their horses to a stop. He turned his horse and rode up beside his two charges. "In order to make decent time, we need to pick up the pace a bit—a gentle trot would be best, time-wise and for the well-being of the horses. Are you both comfortable with such a gait?"

Magdalena and Lazarus nodded.

"Good. We'll trot a while and then slow to a walk and keep alternating. Watch for my commands. If everything goes as planned, we should arrive in Joppa around dawn. Any questions or problems?"

"My legs are going to be so sore after this," said Lazarus with a pained smile. "I'm already feeling it."

Longinus smiled. "Happens to everyone."

He turned his horse again, and they rode off into the night.

——◆≻※≺◆——

JUDEA
THE SEA OF GALILEE
LAST HOURS BEFORE DARK
33 AD
THE TWENTY-SECOND DAY

Peter was grateful for the company. And to be on a boat again, working with his hands and his muscles, among friends, grateful they had decided to join him. And to be away from his own thoughts.

In addition to Peter's closest circle of friends among the Apostles, Thomas, Bartholomew, and Phillip decided that they, too, wanted to go fishing that night. All seven of them loaded Peter's fishing boat with the necessary provisions and well-mended nets. As experience had taught Peter, the best time to go fishing on the Sea of Galilee was at night. That way, the fish couldn't see their nets and swim around them.

They left the dock at dark and, using the favorable winds, smoothly made their way to a place Peter had always had the best results finding schools of fish, teeming with tilapia. But despite the confidence expressed by Peter, Andrew, James, and John that this night should produce a good catch, they all became more and more frustrated as they continued to catch nothing. The extra hands were certainly pulling their weight, but it wasn't making a difference.

By dawn, they sailed back into sight of their dock. A tall man stood on the shore, apparently waiting for them. As they drifted into earshot, the man asked them, "Have you caught anything to eat?"

"No," they all said, frustrated and annoyed that this stranger seemed to be mocking their obviously empty boat.

Then the stranger said, "I'll bet if you were to cast your nets over the right side of your boat right now, you'd be pleasantly surprised at the results."

Peter and the others moaned with exhaustion and irritation. "We haven't had any luck fishing for the whole night," he said to the stranger. "What makes you think there's any fish here, so close to shore?"

"It's worth a try, isn't it?" said John. "We've got nothing to lose and this stranger may have seen something we missed."

Peter took a deep breath and sighed. "Okay, John. But I'm only doing this for you, 'Good and Faithful Servant' that you are."

"That's fine," said John, smiling. "If we catch nothing, I'll clean-up the boat."

Slowly but surely, they cast their nets off the right side. Quite quickly, the boat dipped to that side, threatening to roll over. Most of the Apostles moved to the opposite side to offset the possibility of the boat capsizing.

"What's going on?" shouted James.

"We've got fish!" Peter shouted. "Lots and lots of fish!"

The rest of the Apostles pulled at the nets, but it took all of them to finally haul the whole catch onto the deck.

"Look," said John, pointing at the stranger. "It's Jesus!"

"Jesus?" Peter muttered, still struggling with the nets.

Then he saw. It was Him—the man who had loved him; the man who had forgiven him. He dropped the nets, stood, tucked in his clothes, jumped into the water, and began walking to shore.

"Where are you going?" said James.

"It's our Lord!" answered Peter. "I'm not going to keep Him waiting!"

When Peter arrived ashore, where Jesus stood, He had started a charcoal fire with fish and bread cooking.

"Hello Peter."

"My Lord."

"Please, sit. Warm yourself by the fire."

Peter did as Jesus said.

"You have questions."

"We all do, my Lord."

Jesus sat quiet for several minutes, then said, "Why don't you bring me some of the fish you caught?"

Peter stood and found that his clothes had dried completely. He walked back to the water and helped the others drag all the nets and fish onto shore. The others began counting the fish—153 large tilapia—and none of the nets had been torn from the huge catch.

"Come, have some breakfast," Jesus called to them.

The seven Apostles came over and sat by the fire. Their Teacher took the bread and gave it to them, and in like manner the fish. Silently, they sat on the shore and ate, no one daring to speak.

When they had finished breakfast, Jesus tapped Peter's shoulder and nodded to him to come with Him. They stood and Jesus headed up the beach, tossing stones into the water. Peter grabbed a few pebbles off the ground and followed suit. When they had gone just out of earshot of the other disciples, Jesus stopped and looked Peter squarely in the eye, an expression of deep love on His face. He said to Peter, "Do you love me more than these?"

Peter said to Him, "Yes, Lord, you know that I love you."

"Then please, feed my lambs." After a minute, Jesus then asked Peter a second time, "Do you love me?"

"Yes, Lord, you know that I love you!"

"Then please, tend my sheep." After they had walked a little further, He asked again, "Do you love me?"

Peter was distressed that He had asked him a third time. "Lord, you were sent by the Father; you know everything. You know that I love you!"

"Then please, feed my sheep."

Jesus put a hand on Peter's shoulder, then turned back toward the fire. As they neared the other disciples, Jesus spoke loudly, for all to hear.

"Amen, amen, I say to you, when you were younger, you used to dress yourself and go where you wanted; but when you become old, you will stretch out your hands, and someone else will dress you and lead you where you do not want to go." Then Jesus said to Peter, "Follow me," and began to walk the other way, away from the shore.

Peter thought Jesus said this to the Apostles there to indicate by what kind of death Peter would glorify God. He thought of Judas, then shook the thought from his head. Peter heard something behind them, then turned and saw John following.

Peter said to Jesus, "Lord, what about him?"

Jesus said, "What if I want him to remain until I come back? What concern is it of yours? But right now I want you to follow me."

As they passed his boat, Peter turned out of habit to see if it needed more cleaning to be ready for its next run, but then when he looked back to where Jesus had been walking and talking, He had vanished.

He was alone again. In the dark. He still had questions.

JERUSALEM
THE ROAD TO JOPPA
JUST AFTER MIDNIGHT
33 AD
THE FOURTEENTH DAY

They had ridden for about another hour when Longinus held up his arm for everyone to stop. Mary Magdalene could see that they were part-way up a long incline. Straight ahead, the road wound upward toward much higher ground. To the southwest, she could see the brightly lit city of Jerusalem with its golden walls and gleaming temple.

"The reason we've stopped," Longinus began, "is so I can explain what might lie ahead. Pretty soon we'll pass through more heavily wooded areas, along with chest-high bushes and heavy undergrowth—ideal for wild boars and brown bears. Most of the time, these animals mind their own business and would much prefer to be left alone. But, if somehow they feel threatened by our presence..." His meaning was clear.

"What are we supposed to do if they come after us?" Magdalena asked.

"Exactly what I tell you," said Longinus.

"Have you had to fight them before?" asked Lazarus.

Longinus nodded slowly. "Mostly, you should just stop and remain still until I tell you. I'll be doing my best to distract them if they approach, and they'll most likely leave you alone as long as you and your horse remain still and quiet." He studied them for a moment. "If there's serious danger, expect to hear me shout, 'Freeze.' That's probably all I'll have time for."

He then turned his horse and began to trot up the incline.

They rode on again for about an hour and reached the top of the hill before beginning their descent. Below, they could see the shimmering lights of Joppa with the Mediterranean and Cyprus barely visible beyond. The moonlight shone through the clouds and lit the fishing and ocean-going vessels as they bobbed and strained with the mild pre-dawn breeze.

As they continued their descent toward Joppa, Longinus announced, "We're now entering Sharon Plain, one of the most productive agricultural sites in all Israel."

"And that's important to know because . . .?" said Lazarus.

"Because it's where wild animals like to hunt at this time of night—their food sources here are almost limitless."

Across the road less, than 300 feet ahead, Magdalena spotted a family of wild boars prancing through the brush.

"Freeze," said Longinus.

Magdalena did as she was told and she heard Lazarus do the same. They watched in silence as the wild pigs made their way toward a heavily wooded area, filled with closely bunched waist-high bushes.

A few minutes passed before Longinus gave the "all clear" signal.

When they had ridden about half the distance to where the boars had crossed, Longinus shouted, "Freeze!"

He had barely uttered the word when Magdalena spotted a growling brown bear and her two cubs lumbering across the road, right where the wild boars had crossed. The bears were running in the same direction as the wild boars.

"Looks like it's breakfast time," murmured Lazarus.

"That's nature's way," said Longinus.

He waited a few minutes, and then they heard loud squealing and growling coming from the wooded area.

"Let's get out of here," said Longinus, kicking his horse. "Quickly."

All three mounts had just begun breaking into full gallop when one large wild boar came running straight at Longinus. "Freeze!" he shouted, taking immediate evasive action with his horse and galloping the black steed toward the opposite side of the road, the boar in pursuit. While Longinus directed his galloping mount with his legs, he simultaneously undid the netting apparatus attached to the back of his saddle, and shook it out into what looked like large fish netting with a rope attached to one end.

Magdalena and Lazarus could do nothing but remain completely frozen in place.

Their guide stopped his horse and ran one end of the rope

around a strong tree and attached it to his saddle. As the boar closed, Longinus tossed the netting over the rushing boar and spurred his Arabian away from the tree. The netting fell over the boar and trapped him inside. Still atop his horse, Longinus cinched the net and tied off the trap by securing the other end around another tree, tying it in a tight knot, and cutting the unused rope, so as to retain control of the rest of the long rope.

Realizing that he was caught, the boar squealed, thrashing and roaring as if he had been stabbed. Attracted by the noise, the brown bear came clumping up the incline toward where the boar bucked and screamed. The bear bellowed and snorted, a warning to anyone in her path.

Longinus reined his black horse hard downhill and kicked for it to move quickly out of the bear's way. Then the bear stood up, becoming a roaring colossus. Longinus' horse reared into attack position, trumpeting with front feet flailing. Both feet struck the bear right in his face, knocking the bear off balance, but as it fell to ground, its teeth found Longinus' left leg and foot while its extended claws slashed the man's left side. Beneath him, the Arabian squatted down on all fours and turned its hind quarters toward the bear; the steed launched two brutal rear kicks to the bear's chest and head, temporarily stunning her.

Longinus waved at Lazarus and Magdalena to follow him away from the animals and they wasted no time following his command, galloping their horses as fast as they could, trying desperately to catch up to Longinus and put as much distance between them and the bear as possible. Once he had raced far enough ahead, he slowed the Arabinan to a stop so he could inspect his wounds.

They were just a few miles from Joppa.

Magdalena slowed her horse, as did Lazarus behind her. Longinus had blood running out from his left shoulder, down his arm, and to the bottom of his foot. It looked black in the moonlight.

His boot had been torn open and had blood dripping to the ground. His horse had blood on his legs and neck. Magdalena could see that Longinus was in great pain. He wobbled a little.

Afraid he might pass out any moment, Magdalena grabbed a waterskin from her saddle and tossed it to Lazarus, who was still catching his breath.

"Get up on his horse behind him and pour water over his head and neck," she said, dismounting. "It's not much, but we need to clean the wounds as best we can." She walked over to Longinus. "How bad is it, soldier?"

"I can make it to Joppa," Longinus whispered, his breath heavy. "I just need to check the left front leg of my horse."

"Oh no you don't," she said, stopping him from dismounting. "If you get off that horse and you lose your strength, I won't be able to get you back on." She began removing some of her outer garments. "Lazarus, let him hold the water and slide off his horse. I need your help." The young man seemed to be in a state of semi-shock, but he was doing as she told him. "Lazarus!" He turned to look at her as she continued to remove extraneous articles of clothing. "You can do this. Now, I need you to help me stop the bleeding. I'll need whatever garments you can spare."

Together, they wrapped the soldier's left arm and leg as best they could and held the make-shift bandages tight in place with the rope he still had attached to his saddle. They did likewise for his horse.

When they were done, Mary told Lazarus to get back up on the Arabian. "You need to hold him close and firm so he doesn't fall off. He may yet pass out. We're going to have to walk the horses slowly. His horse is limping, but I think he'll make to Joppa and the family that's waiting for us."

"I'll be holding on," Longinus said.

"I know you will, Longinus," she said. "Lazarus, I'll tie your horse to his and lead both. Whatever happens, make sure he stays on the horse, okay?"

Lazarus nodded. "He's pretty big, you know. But I'll do my best."

"That's all God asks," she said, mounting her chestnut. She took a deep breath and urged her horse forward, slowly, toward Joppa.

CHAPTER SIXTEEN

JUDEA
CITY OF JOPPA
DAWN
33 AD
FIFTEENTH DAY

*I*n accordance with the arrangements Joanna and Susanna had made with the Arimathea family, Joseph had ordered a lookout posted at the entrance to the shipyards for a party of three—two males, one female. He knew to look for riders on horseback, but had no idea that one of the men would be a Roman soldier, bandaged nearly head-to-foot and covered in blood.

Fortunately, Joseph recognized the woman. "Mary! Mary!" he called out as the three bedraggled riders entered the Joppa shipyards. "Sweet mercy. What's happened?"

She could barely find the strength to nod and acknowledge his question.

"We need a doctor and a clean place to care for this man's wounds," she murmured as loud as she could manage. "He's been attacked by a bear and lost too much blood."

"My word." Joseph turned, placed two fingers in his mouth, and blasted out a powerful whistle. Within seconds, several people came running from a big ocean-going ship that had *Mother Mary* painted on its stern. "Thank you for coming so quickly," Joseph said as they came within earshot. "We need ship's doctor right away."

His son David turned on his heel and ran back toward the ship. "I'll get him!" he shouted over his shoulder.

Joseph pointed and said, "We need to move this man to our ship where our doctor can properly tend to his injuries."

The ship's crew began to remove the wounded soldier from the younger man's tight grip.

"What's his name, Mary?" Joseph asked, holding the reins for Mary's chestnut.

She slowly dismounted and took a deep breath. "His name is Cassius Longinus. If it weren't for him, we would undoubtedly have been killed long before we got here. Don't you recognize him from Golgotha?"

"Golgotha? What are you talking about?" Joseph looked at the bloody soldier closely. "I don't recognize him at all."

"Picture him on that same horse, only in a Roman display uniform."

Joseph's face sank into a scowl. "You mean the centurion who supervised the crucifixion of Jesus? This is the same man?"

Mary Magdalene nodded.

Joseph let out a bitter laugh and gave more instructions to those who had come running in answer to his whistle. He shook his head at Magdalena in disbelief. "Clearly I've missed quite a few developments. Let's talk later, once we've tended to their needs. Is the young man injured?"

"No, just Longinus. The other one is most likely in shock from the whole ordeal. He's the one the chief priest wants murdered—his name is Lazarus."

Joseph nodded and took pains to be sure both men—the one in the saddle and the one behind—were carefully lowered off the bloodied Arabian onto a strong carrying blanket.

When the reception party had finally begun their way back toward the ship with both men in tow, Joseph turned to Mary and said, "You know, I spent nearly my whole life in this part of the world. I thought it would pain me to leave where so many memories still live. But now that we're here, I find myself feeling quite happy. It will be a great relief to be free of all the scandal, atrocities, and depravity that has infested Jerusalem and its Temple."

Again he shook his white-haired head. "This city used to be such a shining, blessed place, but they've turned it into a bloody snake pit."

❖

JUDEA
MT. TABOR IN GALILEE
MID-MORNING
33 AD
THE TWENTY-FIFTH DAY

The seven apostles who had gone fishing together on Peter's boat pitched their tents at the foot of Mt. Tabor and were soon joined by the other four: Matthew, Simon, James of Alphaeus, and Thaddeus. Discussion soon broke out and Simon the Zealot again voiced his revolutionary opinion of Jesus and His ministry—that Jesus would ride into view at any moment astride a huge war horse, leading a vast army of heavenly warriors that would attack Jerusalem and crush their Romans oppressors. Peter shared a glance with James and John and rolled his eyes.

Simon noticed. "What's going on?" he blurted. "Our brothers Peter, James, and John have been unusually quiet while the rest of us are struggling to make sense of recent events." Turning to Peter, he said, "Why are you three so quiet?"

Peter looked at James and John, and said, "Is this the right time?"

James and John looked at each other, then nodded at Peter. James said, "I think this is the time that Jesus intended."

"What are you talking about?" Simon said.

"Please just listen," said James.

Simon extended his hand, welcoming Peter to proceed uninterrupted. Peter looked at the others for objections, and hearing none, began.

"Remember when we went with Jesus to the region of Caesarea Philippi and He said to all of us, 'There are some standing here who will not taste death until they see that the kingdom of God has come into power?'"

"I remember that," said Andrew. "Why is that important now?"

Peter scratched his head. "Because six days later Jesus took James, John, and myself and led us up a high mountain—just the three of us. When we reached the top, He changed. He looked like a different person and His clothes became dazzling white—whiter than any garment we had ever seen—glowing, like a summer's full moon. And then, Elijah and Moses appeared and began talking with Him.

"I felt drunk, though I'd not had any wine. And I remember thinking that Jesus wanted us to join in the conversation. But I was terrified out of my wits. We all were.

"So I said, 'Rabbi, it's good that we're all here! Let James, John, and I make a tent for you, Moses, and Elijah.'

"Jesus seemed puzzled at what I had said, or maybe at why I had presumed to speak at all. He didn't respond to my suggestion, or even acknowledge that I had spoken. I couldn't think of anything else to say, and we were all so scared that none of us dared speak again.

"Then a thick cloud came, casting a dark shadow over all of us.

169

And from the cloud came a deep Voice, though it seemed to come from inside our own heads all at once. The Voice said, 'This is my beloved Son. Listen to Him.'

"The three of us nearly fainted. We looked at each other, unsure of whether we had all just heard the same thing. But we had. And in the next instant we were once again alone with our friend Jesus. In His proper body.

"He turned away from us without a word and began walking down the mountain. After a short while, He said to us, 'Do not share what you have just seen and heard with anyone until the Son of Man has risen from the dead.'"

Peter stopped talking and looked into the faces of all his fellow apostles. "So that's why James, John, and I have been so quiet during our discussions. We all promised not to say anything about what happened on that mountain. And, speaking for myself, I've kept extra quiet because I'm not entirely sure what Jesus meant when he said 'risen from the dead.'"

Andrew sighed and said, "Peter, I don't understand you. Why are you making things more complicated than they need to be?"

"Because our Redeemer speaks in riddles!"

"'Risen from the dead' seems pretty straightforward to me," Andrew said. "Someone dies and someone—God—brings them back to life. Like with Lazarus: he died and Jesus brought him back to life. What's the problem?"

"But," said Matthew, "Lazarus came back as himself, like he was just asleep for four days." The ex-tax collector stopped and looked around at the others. "By the way, I haven't seen Lazarus for a while. Anyone know what's happened to him?"

"I haven't seen Martha and Mary either," said James.

"I heard a rumor," said Simon, "that their family went into hiding because Jesus raised Lazarus from the dead. The chief priest didn't like that—can't have anyone more powerful than the priests.

He wants them all dead because they could give witness to Jesus' power and might."

Peter nodded knowingly. "That's exactly my point. Is Jesus like Lazarus—just someone who went to sleep and then woke up? Or is He different?"

"Different how?" said Andrew. "He died and then came back to life. Seriously, what's your problem?"

"My problem, my brother, is that the Jesus we knew while walking around with Him for three years did not enter locked rooms by flowing through its walls and did not change from one version of Himself to another before our eyes. However, the Jesus we have witnessed since His crucifixion is different.

"The Jesus we saw at the Sea of Galilee was not the same Jesus we saw heal the sick and feed thousands from mere morsels of food. The Jesus we saw at the water—at first a total stranger, then became our Teacher talking to us, then became someone complexly different. He then simply vanished into the air."

Peter stopped and glanced around at the others. "Do you see now what I'm talking about?" he whispered. "Which Jesus will we see when we go up this mountain to meet with Him? Will He be the Jesus we knew? Or will He be a refashioned Jesus?"

John took a deep breath. "I don't know the answer to your question, Peter," he said. "But have you ever thought about the possibility that Jesus could be both? The one we walked with and the one who rose from the dead?"

Peter shook his head and became silent.

A voice calling from a distance broke their silence. They looked up the mountain and saw Jesus waving for them to join Him.

"Well," said Peter, "maybe He'll give us a chance to ask Him?"

They all stood and hastened up the mountain to where Jesus waited, unsure of what to expect. Once they got close, each of them silently dropped to their knees and prostrated themselves at His feet, including Peter.

None of the Apostles said a word, though the endless questions they had been discussing still raced through Peter's thoughts.

In silence, Jesus looked down at them on the ground for a few moments and then, without welcoming remarks or explanation, said, "All power in Heaven and on earth has been given to me. Go, therefore, and make disciples of all nations, baptizing them in the name of the Father, and of the Son, and of the Holy Spirit, teaching them to observe all that I have commanded you. And thus, I am with you always, until the end of the age."

Jesus stopped speaking.

The only noise was the wind whipping about the top of the mountain.

"I'll see you here in a week," Jesus said. "Many of your brethren too."

The eleven looked around. Jesus had vanished. There had been no opportunity to ask questions or seek clarification. They were by themselves with just the wind.

CHAPTER SEVENTEEN

JUDEA
CITY OF JOPPA
EARLY MORNING
33 AD
SIXTEENTH DAY

Magdalene slept for 24 hours before she opened her eyes to learn how severely the entire ordeal with Lazarus had sapped her inner reserves. The injuries to Longinus and his horse had been non-lethal. The ship's doctor assured her that without the improvised first-aid she and Lazarus had provided, the outcome might well have been fatal for Longinus and permanently crippling for his horse.

But there was no time for self-congratulation. They were now a day behind schedule.

Magdalena quickly arranged for a horseback messenger to bring a coded message of their safe arrival back to Joanna and Susanna, as well as to Lazarus' sisters, who would no doubt be worried out of their minds by now. Magdalena included in her message that she would be staying on in Joppa for a least another week. She had to ensure the complete recovery of Longinus and his horse—they were her responsibility.

"Your soldier told me he threw the spear into Jesus' side," Joseph said once the messenger had gone. He sat down beside her on the ship's deck, the salty breeze blowing gray hair across his face. "That was barely two weeks past. Why trust him in all this business? You said it yourself: Lazarus is Jesus' legacy."

"God has worked inside Cassius' heart," Magdalena said with a smile. "He voluntarily stood guard outside the Upper Room for an entire day without relief when we were at our most fearful. I trust him with my life... And he entrusted me with his."

"Is that why you're staying? To repay some debt you feel you owe this Roman? My physician is more than capable of caring for him."

"My care will care for him too," she said simply. "I do care for him."

"He helped kill your Redeemer? Why would you care for him?"

"Because Jesus would have cared for him."

Joseph smiled and said nothing.

"You know He would have," Magdalena continued. "Kindness, love, forgiveness—those are Jesus' legacy just as surely as Lazarus is."

"Just as surely as you are, Mary of Magdalene," Joseph said, standing. "You are wise beyond your years and kind beyond any reason you have to be so. We'll keep the boy beneath deck and set sail once you and your soldier have gone. Stay as long as you'd like, but don't forget your appointment in Galilee. Your Jesus will want you there."

She had not forgotten. She still had time.

JERUSALEM
CENACLE HOUSE
MID-MORNING
33 AD
THE TWENTY-FOURTH DAY

Joanna and Susanna also sent messages to the Apostles now making camp in Galilee that Mother Mary felt much better and would be coming with them to the meeting on Mt. Tabor. They were also bringing Martha and Mary of Bethany, but kept that a secret for everyone's safety—they planned to disguise both sisters. Martha and Mary had already made it very clear they would not be stopped from going to Galilee, despite the danger.

The one thing neither Joanna nor Susanna had done yet was bring Mother Mary into the loop as to the imminent peril everyone faced as a result of Caiaphas' fear of young Lazarus. But the time had nearly come for them to depart and the secret could not be kept much longer.

"I don't understand," said Mother Mary, upon hearing of their secret dealings with Mary Magdalene to help Lazarus escape the city. "Why would the high priests want to kill Lazarus? He hasn't done anything to them or anyone."

"But they're afraid that he might," said Susanna.

"Might do what?" Mary said. "Be a moody young man who despises them?"

"Provide irrefutable testimony that Jesus is God," replied Joanna.

The seriousness of the whole ordeal hit Mary visibly and her eyes went wide.

"Your Son brought Lazarus back to life after he'd died and been buried. His death, burial, and resurrection were witnessed by large crowds," continued Joanna. "The Sanhedrin elders can't call that

175

many Israelites liars—but if the problem disappears, quietly and permanently, they can ignore the threat to their power until it's not a threat anymore."

"If you hadn't heard," said Susanna, "the Temple elders have invented a new lie about Jesus: that He didn't rise from the dead, but that His followers stole Him from the grave."

"What makes the Lazarus situation so dangerous," Joanna resumed, "is that the Temple elders now consider Lazarus a far greater threat to their disinformation campaign than Jesus. And if Lazarus were to be killed, then the Chief Priest and his cohorts could invent yet another story and say that the resurrection of Lazarus was nothing more than another zealot hoax."

Mother Mary shook her head, trying to digest all that she had just heard. "Those men of the Sanhedrin have truly lost their way—lost their path to God. They were once blessed by the Father with the gift of deep faith, a faith they had the opportunity to teach and use to bring their people together in grace. But instead, they have squandered their Father's gift, chosen the path of murder and self-serving and vicious tyranny."

"That's exactly right," said Susanna. "And that's why it's so dangerous for you to go to Mt. Tabor to see your Son. Those killers are going to be lying in wait for all followers of Jesus."

Mother Mary nodded her understanding of what she'd just been told.

"Thank you both for being so direct and thoughtful and loving concerning my personal safety, but this isn't the first time I've had to face this kind of danger. The hazards of birthing the Son of God are part of that same territory. Ever since my pregnancy, there have been numerous incidents where Joseph and I have known that our family was in grave danger. We prayed about it and placed ourselves in the hands of God the Father, who always kept us safe. God has a plan for us. He loves us and wants what's the very best for us—all of us. I may be in mortal danger, but those men of the Sanhedrin are in grave danger too—of losing their souls."

Mother Mary slid off her chair onto her knees.

"We need to pray for those men," she said and began reciting the prayer that her Son had taught them. "Our Father..."

JUDEA
CITY OF JOPPA
EARLY MORNING
33 AD
THE TWENTY-FIFTH DAY

By now Magdalene had learned the names of her new body-guards—Noah and Daniel. They were not soldiers like Longinus, but they had helped break Joseph out of prison. They were not much for company, and she missed the assuring presence of her centurion friend. At least Longinus had recovered enough to set sail.

"If Jesus is there when you arrive," he had told her before departing, "tell Him I'm sorry."

"He knows you are," she told him. "And He forgave you before you even realized you were sorry."

Her new bodyguards did not say much.

A young woman who served the Arimathea family had volunteered to accompany Magdalena as well. Her name was Roberta and she had lived in Joseph's family household since her parents' death from consumption some ten years earlier. As a welcome member of the household, Roberta had learned to cook and make sure that those in her care slept and ate well. And by now, she was aware of the dangers that could be lurking along the roads to Mt.

Tabor. But she was not afraid. Roberta was determined to meet the man Magdalena held in such high regard.

Mary Magdalene had given her return journey to her friends a lot of thought and decided that the best route would be Joppa to Caesarea; Caesarea to Jezreel; Jezreel to Tiberias and finally to Mt. Tabor. Barring any unforeseen delays, the trip would take roughly a week, so Magdalena made sure to pack enough food, water, and sleeping rolls.

She had spent enough time walking long distances in her life—before and after she met Jesus—to know how to fall in with other groups headed in the same general direction and pitch camp with them and share in keeping the watch while the others slept. The problem was she had a hard time sleeping when she traveled. For her to get a good night's sleep, she had to be in a bed where she had nothing to worry about—especially hired assassins.

Magdalena well knew how to keep watch though, and always volunteered to take the hardest watch—the one just after midnight. Roberta had surprised her when the girl volunteered to keep watch with her.

"I can't sleep," Roberta said. "This business of having to worry if total strangers may be hiding in wait to kill us makes me think a lot."

"About what?" Mary said.

"About life and death. How quick death can come and how much we take life for granted. Like with my parents. Never got over how quickly it all happened. One minute we were a happy family, and a few weeks later, I was all alone."

"How did you meet Joseph and his family?"

"We lived next door, and I was always over there playing with David's children. They were very kind to me."

Mary nodded. "They're good people."

"Better than 'good people' by thousands of miles!"

Mary laughed. "Thanks for keeping watch with me. It's really nice to have someone to talk with at this hour."

"Yeah, it's good to not be alone," Roberta said with a smile. "Sorry if this isn't the most pleasant topic, but could you please explain to me why people may want to kill us?"

"Of course. You remember the young man at the docks that Joseph and David were keeping below decks?"

"Yeah. Lazarus, right?"

"Yes. Lazarus died. He was in a crypt for four days. Then Jesus brought him back to life. That kind of power is a threat to the High Priests' power if everybody knows about it. They're scared Lazarus will go around telling everyone how Jesus brought him back to life. But if they kill Lazarus, then he can't tell the truth about Jesus."

Roberta nodded and scratched her head. "So what does that have to do with us?"

"If they can capture or kill any friends of Lazarus or his family, then they plan to force people to tell them where Lazarus has gone."

"But you said Jesus rose from the dead too, right?"

"He did," Magdalena said, staring out into the dark night. "He appeared to me. He spoke to me."

"So why doesn't Jesus just appear to the killers and tell them to leave Lazarus and his family alone?"

Magdalena looked into Roberta's eyes. "I don't know. Maybe He will."

Roberta nodded. "I think I want to be alone, so I can pray for Lazarus."

Mary Magdalene smiled. "I think that's a really good idea."

After Roberta left, Magdalena looked up into the clear sky and said a quick prayer of her own. She prayed for strength and vigilance. When she had finished, it occurred to her to set up a "buddy" system for the next day, so two of her group would always keep watch for a few hours and then rotate with the others. That way, no one would have to bear too much loss of sleep.

Just before reaching Caesarea, Noah and Daniel came to Magdalena and asked to speak with her and Roberta in private, away from the others in the caravan they had gotten permission to travel with.

"We're being followed," Noah said.

"We're worried," Daniel said, "because the same Canaan dog has been staying about a half-mile behind us, no matter what pace we keep."

"Last night we went looking to see where the dog slept," said Noah, "but it was nowhere to be found. Its owner obviously hides the dog at night or when resting."

Mary scratched her head. "And this is important to us because . . .?"

"Thank about it," said Noah. "It's a clever way to follow us. The dog looks very ordinary and non-threatening. They give it your scent and it follows wherever you go, but from a distance. Those watching the dog work in shifts out of view so it's impossible to figure out who its masters are."

Magdalene listened carefully, frowning the whole while.

"So what if the dog does follow us?" she said. "It's not going to stop us from getting to Mt. Tabor. And once we get there, the dog's also going to arrive, and then we can introduce it and its handlers to Jesus. I'm sure our Lord would be happy to provide the canine with some fresh fish."

Noah and Daniel broke into loud laughter, and Mary couldn't help but smile.

"Please don't misunderstand," she said. "I very much appreciate how alert you both are to the danger. It's a weight off my shoulders to not have to worry about every little thing, and what you two noticed about the dog following us is a very big thing. But I believe that for the time being, we're fine. If the dog and its masters start to get closer, then we will re-examine our strategies."

They had just left the village Jezreel and were heading north toward Tiberias when Noah and Daniel came to Mary Magdalene again and wanted to speak in private.

"That dog's now less than a quarter of a mile behind us," said Noah.

"Are we ready to go into 'defensive' mode?" asked Daniel.

Magdalena took a deep breath. "Well, I don't want to panic just yet. But it wouldn't hurt for you to set up that netting we brought and get it ready—just in case."

Daniel and Noah looked at each other and nodded.

"I can't wait to see the look on those men's faces when we go 'defensive'," said Daniel.

"I just feel sorry for that dog," said Noah. "It's never going to know what hit it."

Mary looked sad. "I don't want us to hurt the dog if we can avoid it. I just want to make sure it can't follow our scent anymore. The dog's just trying to please its owners. If we knew who they were, we could do something different. But for the moment, just stay alert and keep an eye on that dog."

Noah and Daniel looked at each other and shrugged.

"Whatever you say," said Daniel.

"I don't understand," said Noah.

Mary sighed. "Someday you will."

JUDEA
MT. TABOR IN GALILEE
MID-MORNING
33 AD
THE THIRTY-SECOND DAY

At the foot of an oak tree, Peter watched with growing appre-
hension as endless columns of families and their friends trudged
up Mt. Tabor. He carefully studied the many followers of Jesus
who were now picking out places to rest and wait; he couldn't believe how many of them he'd never seen before. He could see that
some had traveled great distances, but there were a few who had a
strange aura about them—an air and karma that made Peter wonder if they really were followers of Jesus. They spent too much time
nervously glancing about—for whom or what, Peter could not dis-
cern. But the menace of the assassination teams sent for Lazarus,
his family, and friends seemed a likely possibility.

Peter prayed that was not the case.

He had left his tent and walked to the top of Mt. Tabor long
before dawn so as to pray alone, away from the endless noise of the
crowds and the distractions of the other ten Apostles. He wanted
peace and quiet to think through what he really believed about
Jesus, and what he thought Jesus had in mind for him.

The last words Jesus spoke to him about "feeding His sheep"
bounced endlessly around in his thoughts. But he kept stumbling
over the same three questions: Which Jesus was the real Jesus?
What happened to the Messiah that Israel had been promised for
hundreds of years? And how could Jesus have forgiven him?

By the time the first groups of followers worked their way to
the mountain top, Peter had finally concluded that Andrew had
it right. Jesus could simultaneously be more than one version of
Himself. After all, Jesus was God made flesh, so it made no sense

for Peter to think of limiting what God could or could not do or how many different forms of Himself He may decide to show at any one time. Human logic didn't apply to a being who could conquer death and change His appearance at will.

And about the Messiah issue, Jesus was certainly the Messiah, just not the Hero Messiah their people been expecting for so many centuries. The whole idea of an earthly Hero Messiah like King David had been so heavily pounded into his thinking since childhood and well into his adult years that it just never occurred to him that any other kind of Messiah could be possible. This gap in understanding was again due to the limits of his human thinking. But a paradise here on earth, in this life, was all he had ever dared hope for.

Paradise after death, as Jesus had described, held little space in Peter's reality. Such blessings were surely reserved for the most holy of men. And that was not him. Peter knew who he was—the son of a fisherman going back several generations. His work was simple, wholesome, and honest. It provided for him and his family. Beyond that, Peter had given little thought to what happened once he died.

But then Jesus came into his life and started talking about His kingdom, but it wasn't of this world. This had sent Peter reeling into serious questions of his beliefs—as well as his sanity. He knew he didn't want to go to the netherworld, and staying out of that place, he thought, would happen if he remained honest and trustworthy for the rest of his days. But how could there be a kingdom filled with joy and love and harmony that existed after death? A Messiah with a kingdom more wonderful than anything King David had ever built? And what did Jesus mean when He said that kingdom was at hand?

There was also the problem of Jesus' forgiveness. That too made no human sense. All his life, his parents, family, and friends talked about forgivable and unforgivable deeds. Most misdeeds were forgivable—being late, forgetting to do something that had been assigned, looking sloppy, lack of personal cleanliness, occasionally drinking too much, losing one's temper with family and friends, expecting too much of others, and forgetting to compliment those deserving of appreciation.

But some misdeeds far exceeded acceptable behavior and were unforgivable—lying, breaking a trust or solemn promise, cheating on one's spouse, striking one's spouse or children, and abandoning someone in need. So how could he possibly accept Jesus' forgiveness? How could he forgive himself? He thought he had made peace with this forgiveness so many times since Jesus' death, but the shameful ache in his heart remained, along with a nagging thought that would not leave his head—he had committed an unforgiveable act toward someone he loved with all his heart.

"What are you doing?"

It was the voice of his brother Andrew that interrupted his thoughts. "We've been looking for you. Did you tell anyone you were here?"

Peter stood up and they exchanged a brotherly hug.

"No, I did not tell anyone," Peter said. "I'm sorry if I caused you and the others worry. I left before dawn and didn't want to wake any of you."

Now John and James joined them. "Do we need a bath, Peter?" said James. "Is that why you left while the rest of us were sleeping?"

Peter smiled warmly and clapped him on the back. "Yes, I've been meaning to speak to you about that, James. Not only do you need a bath, but let's talk about your snoring!"

They all laughed.

"Have any of you noticed," said John, "that there are a lot of new followers here today? At least a dozen or so. And they all look like they lift dead fish barrels for a living. Does anyone besides me think that we may see an unprovoked attack by men hunting for Lazarus?"

Andrew cleared his throat. "You know, John, it's equally possible that those 'new' men are here to help keep the peace. Isn't it completely possible that one of our benefactors has hired some strong men to help make sure we're all safe and that nothing like what you just mentioned actually happens?"

John shrugged. "I suppose it's possible. Ever the optimist, Andrew. I pray you're right."

Just then Joanna and Susanna and their friends came into view and joined the four Apostles. The two women were leading a small caravan of donkeys with female riders—all dressed to look like old women. Everyone began hugging and laughing—Mother Mary, Martha and Mary of Bethany, Mary of Zebedee, Clopas and Mary of Emmaus, Mary Mark and her husband and son, as well as Joanna and Susanna.

Looking around, Mother Mary scowled. "I don't see Mary Magdalene," she said. "Joanna and Susanna told me she would be here. Does anyone see her? I haven't seen her in weeks."

"You're right," said Peter. "I haven't seen her for a long time either."

"She'll be here," said Joanna, looking past their heads. "You can bet on it."

The others turned to where Joanna was looking. Magdalena was walking toward them. She was smiling, pleased to see them all, but her face was sweaty and she had bags beneath her eyes. Close behind came two tall, thick men leading a packhorse donkey, followed by a young girl, carrying a scrip and walking rod.

They all ran to Magdalena and began greeting her with hugs, kisses, and shrieks of delight.

"Where have you been?" Mother Mary said. "I've missed you."

Magdalena grinned with delight. "And I've missed you too. I'm sorry I was gone so long, but I had some important business to take care of. But that's all done and forgotten; I don't have to worry about that anymore."

"Oh good," Mother Mary said, giving her an extra hug. We have much to discuss."

Suddenly a lull and hush came over the mountain top. Peter took a deep breath and, in that moment, truly forgave himself. The guest of honor had arrived.

When Jesus saw the large number of people—over 500—who had gathered at the top of the mountain, He went up among them and sat down. His Apostles and disciples gathered around, but He looked past them to the multitudes. They all followed His example and sat.

"Peace be with you," He said.

And when He said this, He stood and many in the crowd rejoiced and shouted with joy because they could now see Him—many for the first time since His resurrection, many for the first time ever. But some became scared, convinced they were seeing a ghost.

He said to them, "Why are you troubled? Why do questions arise in your hearts? Look at my hands and my feet, they are mine. Touch me and see, because a ghost does not have flesh and bones as you can see that I have."

And as He said this, He showed them his hands and feet. While the multitudes were still incredulous and filled with amazement, He asked His disciples, "Have you anything to eat here?"

Someone handed Him a piece of fresh bread.

He took and ate it in front of everyone assembled.

"Because you have seen me, you have believed; blessed are those who have not seen and yet believe." Jesus then said to the entire gathering, "Go into the whole world and proclaim my words of kindness, love, and forgiveness to every creature. Whoever believes my words and is baptized will be saved; whoever does not believe will be condemned. These signs will accompany those who believe: in my name they will drive out demons, and they will speak new languages. They will pick up serpents in their hands without injury, and if they drink any deadly thing, it will not harm them. They will lay hands on the sick, and they will recover.

"These are words that I spoke to you while I was still with you, that everything written about me in the Law of Moses and in the prophets and psalms must be fulfilled."

Then He opened their minds to a new understanding of Scripture, as He had to Clopas and Mary of Emmaus, and to the disciples He had appeared to at the Cenacle.

And finally He said to them. "Thus it is written that the Messiah would suffer and rise from the dead on the third day and that repentance, for the forgiveness of sins, would be preached in His name to all the nations, beginning in Jerusalem. You are witnesses of these things. And behold I am sending the promise of my Father upon you.

"As the Father has sent me, so I send you."

Having said this, He turned and began to walk back down the mountain from whence He had come. And then He was gone.

"I can see why you speak so highly of Him," Roberta said to Magdalena.

Magdalena smiled at her. "I'm so glad you decided to come and hear Him speak. He's the best man I've ever known—and much more than that."

Just then, she spotted the large Canaan dog that had been just behind them on the road. The dog was barking happily and jumping up and down with delight at the feet of its master, a tall, thick man in his late twenties. The man was openly weeping after

Jesus had spoken.

Mary Magdalene grinned stupidly and turned to Daniel and Noah. "Now do you understand?"

Daniel and Noah smiled and nodded at her.

"Apologies for our hastiness," said Daniel.

"There is nothing to forgive," she said. "In the future, avoid harm whenever you can, and never assume the worst in others."

The two nodded again.

"He'd be proud of you, you know," Noah said.

"And you," she said, getting up to join the other disciples. "Peace be upon you both."

⊷⧉⊶

JERUSALEM
THE PERSONAL RESIDENCE OF PONTIUS PILATE
EARLY DAWN (LATE FOURTH WATCH)
33 AD
THE TWENTY-FIFTH DAY

Caiaphas, his father-in-law, his sons, and a handful of others from the Sanhedrin had received personal invitations via messenger to be at the governor's home before dawn. These Jewish leaders were more than a little bothered by this alarming stunt.

"I can't wait to give Pilate a piece of my mind," Caiaphas whispered to Annas in one corner of the room. "Who does he think he is, ordering us around like a bunch of military cadets? Just because he's governor doesn't give him the right to treat us like dogs."

"Who *do* I think I am, Caiaphas?" Pilate said to the whole room.

Pilate, Procula, and several of his staff including Chuza, acting Commander of the Palace Guard, had entered the room while Caiaphas was speaking to Annas.

Caiaphas looked as though he'd been bitten by a snake, but said nothing.

"Guess what?" Pilate continued. "I do know who I am." He stared daggers at Caiaphas and Annas for a moment. "Shall we indulge in another of our delightful word games, gentlemen, or shall we get to the point?"

No one spoke.

He smiled like a mother lion playing with a recent kill.

"First of all," he said, scorn oozing from every word, "I would like to thank all of you for making sure Joseph of Arimathea had a successful 'escape' from prison. There was one small incident that almost ruined the entire charade, but fortunately Joseph was a better actor than your people were stupid."

Pilate studied the faces of the others. "Congratulations on your small success, which allowed you esteemed gentlemen of the Sanhedrin to save face with your people while giving me a good reason to spare all of you any further consequence."

He took a deep breath, clenching his cheek muscles. "However, you seem determined to sabotage our good working relationship with one another, as this morning we have a much bigger problem—one where even more lives are at stake.

He looked around the room.

"Anyone care to guess what I'm talking about?"

Each of the men of the Sanhedrin shook their heads "no."

Pilate smiled sarcastically. "This is so much fun. All of you from the Most Holy Sanhedrin standing here in my home at the crack of bloody dawn, pretending you have no idea what's on my mind, praying to your God that I'm both blind and stupid."

Annas cleared his throat. "My Lord, we literally have no idea what you're talking about. Instead of berating us, would you please be so kind as to tell us what you mean?"

Pilate chuckled. "Annas, did you really expect that I wouldn't find out about your contract for the murder of Lazarus and his two sisters from Bethany? Do you truly believe that I'm that uninformed about what happens in Jerusalem?"

Caiaphas and Annas turned pale and sought a place to sit.

"By the way, gentlemen, how's that contract going for you? Have your operatives successfully located their marks and executed their contract?"

He stopped and studied his guests.

"One twenty-five-year-old rich kid who's so confused and useless that his older sisters have to mother him as if he were their own—and yet, nothing. Am I right? Nothing? Nothing in how many days? Let's see—over three weeks now?"

Annas and Caiaphas bowed their heads in shame and embarrassment.

"What's the matter, gentlemen? Cat got your tongue?"

None of the Sanhedrin representatives spoke.

"Well, now it's time for your actions to bear fruit. Since you failed to find or murder anyone from that family in almost a month, looks like it's not going to happen. But," he curled one corner of his mouth, "all is not lost. There's a large gathering scheduled with the recently deceased Jesus of Nazareth on Mt. Tabor.

"And according to all you geniuses, Jesus never arose from the dead, right?" He paused for effect. "That assembly is going to happen in just a few days and a large crowd is expected—maybe 500, possibly more, if my sources are correct."

Caiaphas finally spoke. "We've heard rumors to that effect."

"And I'll bet my finest war horse that your team of hired killers are counting the days and nights until they can also show up at this gathering and have free rein to kill anyone they want."

Pilate stopped and looked all around the room at his visitors. "Anyone care to disabuse me of that notion?"

Silence.

"Well, I've got big news for all you holiest of men. It's never going to happen. None of it. Nothing is going to happen on Mt. Tabor and nothing is going to happen to Lazarus or his sisters or any of their friends. Moreover, as far as the noble Sanhedrin is concerned, there never was a contract—merely ugly rumors. Do we understand each other?"

Annas rose from his seat. "What do you mean, My Lord?"

Pilate laughed. "What do you mean?" he said mockingly, tossing his head. "You know perfectly well what I mean, Annas. But I'll use small words so there can be no misunderstanding my meaning. If anyone—and I mean *anyone*—at that gathering gets frightened or trips and falls or gets a hangnail, I'm going to hold each of you *personally* responsible. If Lazarus or his sisters or their friends get so much as a stomach ache or a stubbed toe, each of you will be in more trouble than you can possibly imagine.

"And just to ensure clarity regarding the personal stakes for all of you, what that means in practical terms is that each of you will be arrested in the middle of the night by me, tried by me, sentenced by me, scourged and whipped by me, mocked in the streets by me, and crucified by me on Golgotha with barely enough time for those who mistakenly admire you to rush you into a tomb before sundown. Is that plain enough for you, Annas?"

At these strong words the men of the Sanhedrin all stood and went into a huddle in the room's furthest corner from Pilate.

Meanwhile, Pilate walked to Procula with a smirk on his face and kissed her cheek. "How am I doing? Did I leave anything out?"

Procula smiled and whispered in his ear, "Kill the contract. Apart from the gathering."

He nodded and turned to the priests, calling out to them, "I don't know what all of you are whispering about, but it's not going to make any difference. You don't like being treated like dogs? Stop acting like them. Here's what's going to happen, and I advise you not forget a word of what I'm about to say.

"First of all, the contract on that family from Bethany is as of this moment null and void. If any aspect of it ever becomes reality, I'm holding all of you personally responsible.

"Secondly, all of you are hereby ordered to make sure nothing—I repeat, nothing—untoward occurs to any of those at that upcoming meeting—then or ever. If anyone at that gathering or their families sustains any accident or mild misadventure, I'm holding each of you personally responsible. There will be no excuses, no explanations—only consequences. You are to ensure the complete safety of all those at that assembly as well as their families."

"But, your Excellency," Annas said, "how can we possibly accomplish what you're asking? Those hired men are independent contractors! We have no control over them, nor do we have any way of reaching out to them to revise their contracts!"

Pilate smiled at Annas like a shark. "Then I'd say you have a problem, Annas. You should have thought of that when you decided to get into the business of assassinating people you don't like. You are not above Roman laws—and you certainly don't get to write your own laws." He kept staring at Annas. "The answer to your predicament is simple: either you make sure that nothing happens or all of you *will* die. Your lives are in your own hands."

He looked around at the others. "Of one thing I'm sure, my dear friends of the Sanhedrin, my servants will have a complete and detailed account of all that happens at that turnout on Mt. Tabor. I hope for all your sakes that I'm pleased."

The governor slowly glanced around the room and at his entourage one more time.

"There being no objections, I think this non-meeting is over. It never took place, and nothing whatsoever happened. A non-event if ever I saw one!"

CHAPTER EIGHTEEN

The Apostles volunteered one of their tents for Mary Magdalene to nap in and she welcomed the chance for some quiet privacy. Roberta gave her physical support as the two slowly made their way down the mountain to where the Apostles had left the tents when they headed up to the mountaintop. Noah and Daniel followed, leading the donkey carrying all their supplies. Joanna and Susanna told all the others who had come with them to take all but one of the donkeys and they would all meet at the Cenacle back in Jerusalem. The two close friends announced that they would be only too glad to remain behind with Mary Magdalene and her companions. Joanna borrowed two more tents from the Apostles so Roberta, Noah, and Daniel would also have privacy to rest and recover.

It was early afternoon before Magdalena stirred from her nap and sat up. Joanna and Susanna had been sitting outside her tent and heard her stirrings.

"Mary, are you awake?" said Susanna, barely above a whisper.

193

"Yes, I'm awake and feeling much better," she said, pulling back the tent's flaps and peering out. "Wow, looks like it's past noon." Seeing both her friends sitting and waiting, she said, "Thank you for being here. You're both most kind."

"Nonsense," said Joanna. "You don't think we waited all this time because we were worried about your health, do you?" She winked at Magdalena. "We want to know everything that's been happening in Joppa with everyone! You've got some explaining to do, Miss Magdalena, and we're not moving a muscle till we've heard it all!"

Magdalene smiled. "What about Daniel and Noah and Roberta?"

"They're still asleep," said Susanna.

Mary pointed to a shading oak tree. "Let's go over there, so we don't wake them."

"By the way," said Joanna, "we sent Martha and Mary back to Jerusalem with the others. They've been spending most of their time at our homes or in the Upper Room. We figured they'd be asking you questions about their brother, and in your condition, we thought it best to postpone that. They know he's safe, and that's all they're really worried about."

"Thank you," said Magdalena. "I know it's been hard for them, having to adjust to the reality that they're never going to see their brother again. You should have seen them when they had to say good-bye before we left for Joppa. My heart nearly broke for them."

After a moment's pause, Magdalene took a deep breath and launched into a detailed narrative about all that had happened—especially the particulars of the confrontation with the boar and the brown bear.

"It's certainly a good thing Longinus was such a stickler for detail," said Joanna, "what with all the protocols Lazarus and you had to observe. Seems as if those military-like precautions turned out to be a gift from God."

"Indeed," said Magdalena with a smile. "In my wildest dreams, I never expected a head-on charge from a boar and a bear at the same time. Longinus was an absolute blessing as our guide—so calm under fire, never losing his head—even though he was bleeding head-to-foot like a stuck pig. And that beautiful warhorse knew exactly what to do in the face a vicious attack—simply incredible. Without Longinus and his steed, Lazarus and I would have surely been mauled and our remains scattered over the hills of Joppa."

Magdalena smiled. "As it was, Lazarus and I had to strip our outer clothes into bandage strips, doing our best to slow the blood loss from both Longinus and his horse. Lazarus had to get up on Longinus' horse and hold the man tight enough that he would not fall off if he lost consciousness.

"Luckily, Joseph was on watch when we arrived in Joppa. He and the whole shipyard had already been on alert for the possibility of an attack by Caiaphas' forces. Joseph's son David had brought news of the contract just before we arrived.

Magdalena paused and Joanna handed her an animal skin of fresh water.

"So what happened to everyone?" asked Susanna.

Magdalena thought for a moment. "Well, I'm not really sure. What I do know is that Joseph and Lazarus and Longinus left Joppa when I did, all in reasonably good health. Their first stop was Cyprus and, from there, Lazarus could decide on a destination anywhere in Europe, though I think he may have mentioned Africa as well…"

"Good for them," said Joanna. "We actually have some news that we received just before leaving Jerusalem: seems Pilate told Caiaphas and his friends that the contract for Lazarus, his family, and friends was null and void, and if any harm befalls any of us, the governor will hold the Sanhedrin personally responsible—under penalty of death."

Magdalena nearly spit out her water laughing. "Really? Did Procula give you that?"

Susanna and Joanna nodded.

"So, why wasn't she here today?"

"Pilate wouldn't let her," said Susanna. "He feared there might be some violence. He doesn't trust the Sanhedrin anymore—not since they hired that Pagan crowd."

Magdalena shook her head and looked down. "I don't blame him." She took a deep breath and a long sip of water. "Let me tell you a story about a dog—a Canaan dog—one that I will forever see in my dreams."

She stopped and noticed that Roberta, Daniel, and Noah were awake and looking about.

"Actually, I'll tell you about the dog a little later," she said. "I have a feeling we should pack up and be on our way back to Jerusalem."

JERUSALEM
EARLY **A**FTERNOON
33 AD
THE **T**HIRTY-**T**HIRD **D**AY

The journey from Mt. Tabor to Jerusalem measured approximately 60 miles, which required several days and nights of travel, depending on how fast people had the strength and stamina to proceed. The 500 plus followers of Jesus who had come together on the mountain arrived in greatly different groups and rates of speed, but their return trip would, for most, take much longer. There was much to think on, and much to discuss.

On their way back, the eleven Apostles fell into their usual groupings of four, except for the one that had once included Judas. Peter, Andrew, James, and John liked traveling long distances together because they had so much in common and had known each other for many years before any of them met Jesus.

Several days had passed since they left Galilee, but there was still a heavy tension in the air. Something was bothering Peter. Out of compassion for their friend and acknowledged leader, the others kept mostly quiet. They knew without having to be told that Peter was still wrestling with something.

"So," John began, having waited as long as he could. "Would you like to talk about what's on your mind, or would you rather we just leave you alone to work out this problem inside your own head—by yourself?"

Peter sighed. "I don't know what I want. One minute I feel like I need to hear all your feedback, and the next minute I'm thinking it's unfair to burden each of you with my problems. Jesus forgave me. I've even forgiven myself. Truly, I have. But what's got me running in circles is... I can't get comfortable with that forgiveness. Not without penance. Andrew and I were raised a certain way. If we committed an unforgivable act, we would need to show our sorrow through some consequence that would usually cause us great pain and suffering, but also show the sincerity of our request to be forgiven."

"Exactly right," said Andrew. "If we told a lie or broke our word, Dad would make sure we suffered, a *lot*, before he would tell us we were forgiven."

"But Jesus isn't your earthly father," James said. "He's God the Father in Heaven, Creator of everything—including the sun and moon and everything else in between. If God wants to forgive you for something you did wrong, He simply says you're forgiven and that's the end of it. It's as if it never happened. The whole point is that there doesn't *need* to be a punishment! That's the kind way to forgive someone! That's how Jesus taught us to show radical love for one another! I really don't understand your problem."

John chuckled and took a deep breath. "James, it's his problem. He doesn't need our permission to have a problem." He stopped and looked at Peter. "Let me see if I've got this right... You think God is letting you off the hook too easily—that since what you did was *so* unforgivable, you'd feel better if God punished you somehow for denying Him and running away when He needed you. That close to the mark?"

Peter nodded and smiled. "Bullseye. I couldn't have said it better. I do feel as if God's being too easy on me by just saying He forgives me without any severe consequence."

"Jesus never did anything without a reason," John said. "He also charged you with being the 'rock' upon which He would build His church. He told you three times to 'feed His sheep.' Do you for one minute think that either one of those commands are going to be easy? Actually accomplishing those tasks will be the hardest consequence you'll ever have to face. I promise you, there will be nothing easy about what lies ahead for you and His Church. Don't fool yourself into thinking you didn't receive a penance—quite the opposite."

Peter just stared at John. After a few moments, he said, "I hadn't thought of that. Thank you, John, my good friend. What you said has been most helpful."

They walked on in silence for a mile or so before Andrew cleared his throat loudly. "I've got something to say about your problem, Peter."

"What is it?" Peter said. "I'd love to hear."

"This business of God forgiving you when *you* think you don't deserve it," Andrew began, "makes it seem as though you're setting yourself above God."

The others frowned at Andrew.

"What are you talking about?" Peter protested. "There's no way in the world I'm setting myself *above* God!"

"Really?" said Andrew. "Aren't you saying that God needs to ask *your* permission to forgive you, especially if He doesn't demand some sort of harsh consequence?" Andrew looked around at John and James who were now visibly upset.

"Bear with me, while I try to create a somewhat similar example, "Andrew said. "Suppose I got really angry at Peter while we were out fishing—so angry I stabbed him with a knife on purpose. And suppose, Peter didn't die, and Jesus was with us in the boat. So, I immediately apologized to Peter and begged his forgiveness. But Peter remained angry at me and wouldn't respond, so I turned to Jesus and asked His forgiveness. And suppose Jesus said, 'Of course, Andrew, you're forgiven. I know you're truly sorry and would never do it again.'

"But now Peter is really angry at the both of us—Jesus and myself. So does that mean that Jesus should have to ask Peter's permission in order to be able to forgive me?"

No one spoke for several minutes as they walked on.

Tears began to roll down Peter's cheeks.

"What's the matter," asked Andrew. "Did I hurt your feelings? I'm sorry if I did. I didn't mean to. I was just trying to give you my thoughts."

Peter put one arm around Andrew's shoulder. "No, you didn't hurt my feelings, my wonderful brother. But you did make me see something I hadn't seen before. My refusal to welcome Jesus' forgiveness of my misdeeds is wrong. If Jesus chooses to forgive me, then I'm a fool not to accept that forgiveness just because I find it so difficult to forgive myself. Thank you, my brother. And thank you all for your kind patience with me."

John smirked briefly. "You know, Peter, if you still want some penance, you can carry my bags the rest of the way to Jerusalem."

"And, mine too!" said James.

"And mine!" said Andrew.

All four Apostles roared with laughter as they continued their return journey home—all overflowing with the love and joy that Jesus had taught them to embrace.

<hr />

JERUSALEM
EARLY AFTERNOON
33 AD
THE FORTIETH DAY

Mary Magdalene, Joanna, Susanna, Roberta, Noah, and Daniel were the last to return to Jerusalem. The last three proceeded directly to the Arimathea household, where they knew they would be welcomed and given enough time and space for badly needed rest and recuperation.

Magdalena, Joanna, and Susanna went straight to the Cenacle, where they knew many people with questions awaited. For several minutes it seemed like sheer joyful chaos as everyone greeted and hugged and kissed each other in friendship and camaraderie, now that all of them were together and safe once again.

Mary Magdalene held her arms in the air and said, "I'd like all of you to hear me. I have something to say."

The entire Upper Room quickly hushed.

"I wanted to share something with each of you," she said, adjusting the animal skin of water around her neck, "so you'll all hear it from me at the same time. I know a lot of you have questions for me and where I've been and what I've been doing these past weeks. I want to start by saying that what you're about to hear from me is all I'm going to say on these subjects—not because I don't love you, but because I love you so very much. In this mixed up world, sometimes the kindest thing someone can do for another is to refrain from needlessly endangering their life. Sometimes that means not divulging certain sensitive information."

She took a deep breath. "So here goes. First of all, while I've been away, I've been taking care of some very important business. That business has been handled and is no longer a concern for me or anyone else. That's all I will say about where I've been and what I've been doing. Suffice to say, I am back and remain in solidarity with all of you. Doing God's work is all that will occupy my mind and heart for the rest of my life.

"Secondly, there's been a lot of rumors going around about Caiaphas and the Sanhedrin's intent to murder Lazarus and his family and his friends and companions. Let me assure you that Lazarus is completely safe, healthy, and under the protection of people who care about him deeply. Also, I have it on reliable authority that the contract for the murder of Lazarus and those close to him has been cancelled and rendered null and void. Permanently. We no longer have anything to fear with regard to our ability to walk the streets of this city in safety—day or night."

She stopped and swallowed down some water, then spoke again. "We have no idea when we will actually see Jesus again, but I'm confident that we will, and soon. On Mt. Tabor, He said, 'And behold I am sending the promise of my Father upon you. As the Father has sent me, so I send you.' It sounds to me that Jesus will soon leave us with just each other and the memory of Him in our hearts. I pray with all my heart that each and all of us can find the path He has for us individually and collectively—no matter how hard it may be."

She paused. "I love all of you—today and always."

Then she sat down.

The room became completely quiet.

And still. Magdalena could feel their anticipation.

Then, as He had before,, Jesus suddenly stood among them.

"Peace be with you," He said. "I'm going to take a short walk out to the Mount of Olives, and I would love it if all of you would come with me."

About an hour later, when they had all gathered together at the Mount of Olives, a few of the disciples asked Him, "Lord, are you at this time going to restore the Kingdom to Israel?"

He answered, "It is not for you to know the times or seasons that the Father has established by His own authority. But you will receive power when the Holy Spirit comes upon you, and you will be My witnesses in Jerusalem, throughout Judea and Samaria, and to the ends of the earth."

And when He had said this, He exhaled into the cool night air and said, "Receive the Holy Spirit. Whose sins you forgive are forgiven, and whose sins you retain are retained, but stay in Jerusalem until you are clothed with power from on high."

When He had said this, as they were looking on, He was lifted up into the air, and a cloud took Him from their sight. While they were still looking intently at the sky, two figures dressed in blazing white garments stood beside them.

"Men and women of Galilee," they said, "why are you standing there looking at the sky? This Jesus who has just been taken up away from you into Heaven will return in the same way as you have seen Him going into Heaven."

There was a momentary silence among all disciples as they saw the figures vanish before their eyes.

Each of them fell to their knees in turn, many of them murmuring prayers under their breath. A breeze swept across the Mount of Olives as the realization dawned on them: they were all alone now.

They would have to carry on the work Jesus had begun on their own. Many began to weep and sob out of a sense of loss and trepidation at the immense difficulties they envisioned.

"It's up to us now," said Magdalena.

"Yes," said Peter. "It certainly is."

JERUSALEM
THE TEMPLE
PENTECOST
MID-MORNING
33 AD
THE FIFTIETH DAY

After nine days of prayer and meditation, Peter knew what he had to do next. When he awakened on the tenth day, they were all in one place together. The time for Pentecost had been fulfilled and Peter knew the time had come, so he wasn't at all surprised when suddenly there came from the sky a noise like a strong driving wind and it filled the entire building in which they were. Then there appeared to them tongues as of fire, which parted and came to rest on each one of them. And they were all filled with the Holy Spirit and began to speak in different tongues, as the Spirit enabled them to proclaim. They were filled with an indescribable joy and burst from the house into the streets of Jerusalem, Peter leading the way. He had never felt an inner peace as he was now experiencing. He threw his head back in glee and hugged his fellow disciples as he made his way through the streets.

Now there were devout Jews from every nation under heaven staying in Jerusalem. At the sound of the disciples' jubilant ex-hortations, they gathered in a large crowd, but they were confused because each one heard them speaking in his own language. They were astounded, and in amazement asked, "Are not all these people who are speaking Galileans? Then, how does each of us hear them in his own native language? We are Parthians, Medes, and Elamites, inhabitants of Mesopotamia, Judea and Cappadocia, Pontus and Asia, Phrygia and Pamphylia, Egypt, and the districts of Libya near Cyrene, as well as travelers from Rome, both Jews and converts to Judaism, Cretans and Arabs, yet we hear them speaking in our own tongues of the mighty acts of God."

They were all astounded and bewildered, and said to one another, "What does this mean? How can this be happening?"

But others said mockingly, "They have had too much new wine."

Peter heard what they were saying and laughed at the thought. Then he stood up with the Apostles and disciples, raised his voice, and proclaimed to them, "You who are Jews, indeed all of you staying in Jerusalem. Let this be known to you, and listen to my words. These people are not drunk, as you suppose, for it is only nine o'clock in the morning. No, this is what was spoken through the prophet Joel: 'It will come to pass in the last days, God says, that I will pour out a portion of my spirit upon all flesh.

"'Your sons and your daughters shall prophesy, your young men shall see visions, your old men shall dream dreams. Indeed, upon my servants and my handmaids. I will pour out a portion of my spirit in those days, and they shall prophesy. And I will work wonders in the heavens above and signs on the earth below: blood, fire, and a cloud of smoke. The sun shall be turned to darkness, and the moon to blood, before the coming of the great and splendid day of the Lord, and it shall be that everyone shall be saved who calls on the name of the Lord.'

"You who are Israelites, hear these words. Jesus the Nazarene was a man commended to you by God with mighty deeds, wonders, and signs, which God worked through Him in your midst, as you yourselves know. This man, delivered up by the set plan and foreknowledge of God, you killed, using lawless men to crucify him.

"But God raised him up, releasing him from the throes of death, because it was impossible for him to be held by it. For David says of him: 'I saw the Lord ever before me, with him at my right hand I shall not be disturbed. Therefore my heart has been glad and my tongue has exulted; my flesh, too, will dwell in hope, because you will not abandon my soul to the netherworld, nor will you suffer your Holy One to see corruption. You have made known to me the paths of life; you will fill me with joy in your presence.'

"My brothers and sisters, one can confidently say to you about the patriarch David that he died and was buried, and his tomb is in our midst to this day. But since he was a prophet and knew that God had sworn an oath to him that he would set one of his descendants upon his throne, he foresaw and spoke of the resurrection of the Messiah, that neither was he abandoned to the netherworld nor did his flesh see corruption. God raised this Jesus; of this we are all witnesses. Exalted at the right hand of God, He received the promise of the Holy Spirit from the Father and poured it forth, as you can see and hear. For David did not go up into heaven, but he himself said: 'The Lord said to my Lord, "Sit at my right hand until I make your enemies your footstool."'

"Therefore let the whole house of Israel know for certain that God has made Him both Lord and Messiah, this Jesus whom you crucified."

Peter turned to Andrew, James, and John who were listening with noticeable admiration at the amazing words coming from Peter, the fisherman, who had now stepped up to lead the Church that Jesus had established. He shrugged his shoulders as if to say, "Where did that come from?" They all laughed, feeling the power within each of them to move ahead in the work before them.

Now when all those assembled heard Peter's words, they were cut to the heart, and they asked Peter and the other Apostles,

"What are we to do, my brothers?"

Peter said to them, "Repent and be baptized, every one of you, in the name of Jesus Christ for the forgiveness of your sins; and you will receive the gift of the Holy Spirit. For the promise is made to you and to your children and to all those far off, whomever the Lord our God will call."

No one in the Temple area that day argued with Peter nor said that any of his statements lacked truth. No one called for his arrest. Instead, they asked him and the other Apostles for guidance. But Peter gave a simple answer to all questions put to him—that they should repent in the name of Jesus for the forgiveness of their transgressions and be baptized, and they would receive the gift of God's peace; that Jesus loved them perfectly and unconditionally and they should embrace that love, embrace His kindness and forgiveness; and having received such remarkable gifts, they should use them to love others in return.

Peter looked around the Temple area, searching for the Apostle John. He wanted to thank him for his great insight. Now, there could be no doubt that what Jesus had commissioned Peter to do would be the most difficult task he would ever face.

Epilogue

𝕿he men and women of this book (except for a few) left a legacy for all humankind of faith, commitment, compassion, and unconditional love. The fact that so few documented details relating to the end of their lives exists is puzzling. What you see below represents the extent of the data from my research—NA (Not Available) means further reliable data not found.

THE APOSTLES:

How the lives of the Apostles ended is clouded in contradictions. Most of what is thought to be true about their lives is based on tradition or educated deductions by historians/anthropologists. One thing all chroniclers seem to agree upon: ten of the original Apostles (not including Judas) died martyrs. That single fact speaks volumes about the conviction each man brought to his mission. Within the Apostles, there were three basic social groupings:

Peter – died 65 AD in Rome, martyred and crucified upside down at his request

Andrew – crucified and martyred in southern Greece, NA

James – died 44 AD, martyred

John – died 118 AD of natural causes

Philip – martyred 80 AD in Hierapolis, Turkey

Bartholomew (Nathanael) –flayed to death in Armenia, Greece, NA

Matthew (Levi) – martyred in Ethiopia, NA

Thomas – martyred in India, NA

James, son of Alpaeus - martyred 38 AD in Jerusalem

Simon the Zealot - missionary to British Isles, martyred there at age 65

Thaddeus, son of James – martyred in Persia, NA

Judas – died by suicide, hanging, in Jerusalem 33 AD

THE DISCIPLES:

Each of those listed below played a significant role in the life of Jesus, His Apostles, disciples, and followers, before and after the Resurrection:

Mother Mary - the Blessed Virgin Mary was 14 when she conceived Jesus; she was therefore 47 years old when Jesus was crucified and buried. According to Anne Catherine Emmerich, an Augustinian nun in Germany, Mother Mary lived in Ephesus at the end of her life [in her 50s] in the same house as the Apostle John. He kept his promise to Jesus [given as He was dying on the cross] that John would take care of Mary for all her days. Accounts report Mary was taken ["assumed"] body and soul into Heaven.

Mary Magdalene – missionary to Ephesus; died in her late fifties of natural causes, NA

Mary Clopas – wife of Clopas and sister to Mother Mary; believed to have died in France of natural causes, NA

Mary of Zebedee - mother of Apostles James and John; in the Eastern Orthodox Church, she is a saint; believed to have gone to Italy as missionary and died of natural causes, NA

Joanna – wife of Chuza, believed to have died of natural causes, NA

Susanna – believed to have died of natural causes, NA

Longinus – Christian missionary to Cappadocia, Turkey; martyred by Roman soldiers, NA

Lazarus - fled to Cyprus; later received appointment by Barnabas and Paul as bishop of Kition [present-day Larnaka], where he lived 30 more years before dying of natural causes. Mary, Martha, and Lazarus of Bethany were recognized as pre-congregational saints of the Catholic Church (when it first organized). In 2021, Pope Francis declared that the feast day for all three would be July 29 and celebrated by the entire Church on that day each year.

Pontius Pilate - appointed prefect [governor] of Judea, Samaria, and Idumea in 26 AD; removed from office 36 AD by Syrian governor Lucius Vitellius; died in 39 AD under questionable circumstances. It is believed by some that he converted to Christianity and was later martyred and canonized. The Ethiopian Orthodox Church considers Pilate a saint.

Procula [wife to Pontius Pilate] – born 6 BC believed to have had a strong friendship with Mary Magdalene, and to have died the same day as Pilate; also believed to have converted to Christianity the same day as her husband.

MEMBERS OF THE SANHEDRIN:

Joseph of Arimathea - born 41 BC; died of natural causes in 45 AD age 86 in England; originally a member in good standing of the Sanhedrin before the death of Jesus; later vilified and ostracized by the Sanhedrin for helping bury Jesus; considered a saint by the Catholic and the Eastern Orthodox Churches.

Nicodemus – considered the highest ranking "teacher" in the Sanhedrin before the crucifixion of Jesus; together with his childhood friend Joseph of Arimathea buried Jesus; later besmirched by the Sanhedrin for his work on behalf of the dead Jesus and eventually banned by that body; was still corresponding with Joseph in 62 AD; believed to have been martyred sometime in the first century; considered a saint by the Catholic and the Eastern Orthodox Churches, NA.

Caiaphas - born 14 BC; died 46 AD of natural causes; served as Chief Priest 18 AD until 36 AD when he was removed from office by order of Syrian governor, Lucius Vitellius.

Annas - born 23 BC, died 40 AD of natural causes; served as Chief Priest 6 BC until 15 AD when he was ordered removed by Valerius Gratus, governor of Judea; survived by five sons and a son-in-law, Caiaphas.

Bibliography

Agreda, Mary of, *The Mystical City of God* (Volume Three),Charlotte, NC, Tan Books, 2006

Aquilina, Mike, *Ministers and Martyrs*, Manchester, NH, Sophia Institute Press, 2015

Baij, Maria Cecilia, O.S.B., *The Life of Saint Joseph*, Asbury, NJ, The 101 Foundation, Inc., 2000

Ben-Sassom, H.H., Editor, *A History of the Jewish People*, Tel Aviv, Dvir Publishing House, 1969

Bock, Darrell L., *Jesus According to Scripture*, Grand Rapids, MI, Baker Academic, 2006

Brown, Raphael (Compiled by), *The Life of Mary as Seen by the Mystics*, Charlotte, NC, Tan Books, 2012

Caldwell, Taylor & Stearn, Jess, *I, Judas*, New York City, Atheneum Publishers, Inc., 1977

Charlesworth, James H., *The Historical Jesus*, Nashville, TN, Abingdon Press, 2008

Crossman, John Dominic & Reed, Jonathan L., *Excavating Jesus: Beneath the Stones, Behind the Texts*, New York City, HarperCollins, 2001

Deen, Edith, *All of the Women of the Bible*, New York City, HarperCollins, 1955

Emmerich, Anne Catherine, *The Complete Visions of Anne Catherine*, Chicago, Catholic Book Club, 2014

Emmerick, Anne Catherine, *Mary Magdalen in the Visions of Anne Catherine Emmerick*, Charlotte, NC, Tan Books, 2011

Emmerick, Anne Catherine, *The Dolorous Passion of Our Lord Jesus Christ*, Charlotte, NC, Tan Books, 2012

Emmerick, Anne Catherine, *The Life of the Blessed Virgin Mary: From the Visions of Anne Catherine Emmerich*, Charlotte, NC, Tan Books, 2011

George, Margaret, *Mary Called Magdalene*, New York City, Penquin Books, 2002

Hansen, Brooks, *John the Baptizer*, New York City, W.W. Norton & Company, Inc., 2009

Hansen, K.C. & Oakman, Douglas E., *Palestine in the Time of Jesus*, Minneapolis, MN, Augsburg Fortress, 1998

Kelly, Matthew, *Rediscover Jesus*, Erlanger, KY, Beacon Publishing, 2015

King, Karen L., *The Gospel of Mary of Magdala: Jesus and the First Woman Apostle*, Williamette, OR, Polebridge Press, 2003

LaHaye, Tim and Jenkins, Jerry B., *John's Story: The Last Eyewitness*, New York City, The Berkley Publishing Group, 2006

Limbaugh, David, *Jesus on Trial*, Washington, DC, Regenery Publishing, 2015

MacArthur, John, *Twelve Ordinary Men*, Nashville, TN, Thomas Nelson, 2002

MacArthur, John, *Twelve Extraordinary Women*, Nashville, TN, Thomas Nelson, 2005

Maier, Paul L., *Pontius Pilate*, Grand Rapids, MI, Kregel Publications, 1968

Malina, Bruce J., *The New Testament World*, Louisville, KY, Westminster John Knox Press, 2001

Martin, James, S.J., *Jesus: A Pilgrimage*, New York City, HarperCollins, 2014

May, Antoinette, *Pilate's Wife*, New York City, HarperCollins, 2007

McBirnie, William Steuart, *The Search for the Twelve Apostles*, Carol Stream, IL, Tyndale House Publishers, Inc., 1973

Moore, Beth with McCleskey, Dale, *The Beloved Disciple*, Nashville, TN, Broadman & Holman Publishers, 2003

O'Reilly, Bill & Dugard, Martin, *Killing Jesus*, New York City, Henry Holt and Company, LLC, 2013

Pagola, José A., *Jesus: An Historical Approximation*, Miami, Convivium Press, 2014

Plus, Raoul, S.J., *The Little Book of the Virgin Mary*, Manchester, NH, Sophia Institute Press,, 2010

Pope Benedict XVI, *Jesus, the Apostles, and the Early Church*, San Francisco, Ignatius Press, 2007

Rice, Anne, *Christ the Lord: Out of Egypt*, New York City, Alfred A. Knopf, 2005

Ring, Bonnie, *Women Who Knew Jesus*, Bloomington, IN, AuthorHouse, 2015

Rose Publishing, Editor, *Rose Book of Bible Charts, Maps & Time Lines*, Peabody, MA, Rose Publishing, 2015

Ruffin, C. Bernard, *The Twelve: The Lives of the Apostles After Calvary*, Huntington, IN, Our Sunday Visitor Publishing, 1997

Senior, Donald & Collins, John J., Editors, *The Catholic Study Bible*, New York City, Oxford University Press, Inc.,1990

Sheen, Fulton J., *Life of Christ*, New York City, Doubleday, 1977

Smith, Kenneth W., *Judas: A Biographical Novel of the Life of Judas Iscariot*, Lincoln, NE, iUniverse, Inc., 2001

Sri, Edward, *Rethinking Mary in the New Testament*, San Francisco, Ignatius Press, 2018

Tribbe, Frank C., *I, Joseph of Arimathea: A Story of Jesus, His Resurrection, and the Aftermath*, Nevada City, CA, Blue Dolphin Publishing, Inc., 2000

Valtorta, Maria, *The Poem of the Man-God* (Volume Five), Italy, Centro Editoriale Valtortiano, 1990

Acknowledgements

This book would not have been possible without the collective co-operation, skill, talent, and caring that has been required to take this book from an idea to its final form. My heartfelt thanks, appreciation, and love to:

My live-in angel—my wife, Kathy—whose endless contributions, tireless skill, amazing talent, and deep compassion have always been there for me and this project. Her ongoing patience, support, and charity have made the difference between an idea and this now-published prayer for all humankind.

My brilliant son, Matt, whose love for me inspired him to lend his incredible editing and storytelling skills to the formation of this literary effort. I pray he realizes how much his hard work and kindness means to me.

Carol Dawson, my dear friend from our college days in Washington, DC: Her willingness to apply her significant editing skills in the midst of so many other conflicting projects in her life has meant more to me than she will ever know.

All the talented, patient, and kind people at Outskirts Press, especially Elaine Simpson. They are the reason I decided to call upon this publishing company a second time.

CPSIA information can be obtained
at www.ICGtesting.com
Printed in the USA
BVHW070330020321
601385BV00006B/176